THE ROCK BLASTER

Henning Mankell

THE ROCK BLASTER

Translated from the Swedish by
George Goulding

MACLEHOSE PRESS
QUERCUS · LONDON

First published in the Swedish language as Bergsprängaren
by Författarförlaget, Gothenburg, in 1973

First published in Great Britain in 2020 by

MacLehose Press
An imprint of Quercus Publishing Ltd
Carmelite House
50 Victoria Embankment
London EC4Y 0DZ

An Hachette UK company

Translation sponsored by

SWEDISH
ARTSCOUNCIL

A CIP catalogue record for this book is available
from the British Library.

ISBN (HB) 978 0 85705 945 1
ISBN (TPB) 978 0 85705 946 8
ISBN (Ebook) 978 0 85705 948 2

1 3 5 7 9 10 8 6 4 2

Designed and typeset in Quadraat by Patty Rennie
Printed and bound in Great Britain by Clays Ltd, Elcograf S.p.A.

Contents

Author's Preface

It has been twenty-five years since this book first saw the light of day. A quarter of a century, that is. I wrote the first part in an apartment on Løkkeveien in Oslo. It was late autumn and cold. I could see the American embassy through the window of the draughty study. There were demonstrations going on outside the building all the time. I used to walk over there between my writing stints. You could still catch the occasional sharp remark from people passing in the street. But they were fewer and less hostile than before. It was already 1972. The Americans were losing their desperate war of aggression in Vietnam.

I remember that autumn clearly. The leaves turning yellow in the Palace Park, the marines outside the embassy gate always grim. But most of all I remember what I was thinking. It was a time of great joy, of great energy. Everything was still possible. Nothing was either lost or settled. Except that the Vietnamese were certain to win. Imperialism was beginning to show signs of strain. The course had already been set, along sufficiently deep and navigable channels. But there were, of course, also indications to the contrary: neither I nor any of my friends seriously believed that we would see South Africa's apartheid system brought to an end in our lifetime.

In retrospect, I can now recognise that we were both right and wrong, as is always the case when one tries to look into the future.

While I sat and wrote this book, I was thinking: with this one, for the first time, I would get into print. Until then I had managed to have bits and pieces published in the newspapers. And some of my plays had been performed. I had been directing in various theatres. That way I could afford to spend a month at a time only writing. Which was what it was all about. The purpose of my life. I could not imagine anything else. What could it otherwise be?

I had made up my mind to try and avoid ever having any of my work rejected. At least any longer texts. Novels, in other words. For that reason, the year before I had torn up a couple of manuscripts which I did not think were good enough. I never submitted them to a publisher. But when this book was eventually finished (the latter part was written in an equally draughty apartment on Trotzgatan in Falun, a small provincial town in the middle of Sweden), I dropped the manuscript into a postbox. In June I received a postcard with a picture of Dan Andersson. Sune Stigsjöö was the head of Författarförlaget at the time. He told me that the book had been accepted and would be published.

It was well received. (As I recall, Björn Fremer's in *Kvällsposten* was the only negative review.) As a result, I began to get subsidies. I could now dispense with some of my bread-and-butter activities.

That is now a quarter of a century ago. I wrote the manuscript on an unreliable old typewriter with Norwegian characters. Today I am composing these lines on a computer which weighs scarcely more than three kilos.

Certainly, much has happened in those twenty-five years. Some walls have come down, others have gone up. One empire has fallen, the other is being weakened from within, new centres of power are taking shape. But the poor and exploited have become even poorer during these years. And Sweden has gone from making an honest attempt at building a decent society to social depredation. An ever-clearer division between those who are needed and those who are expendable. Today there are ghettos outside Swedish cities. Twenty-five years ago they did not exist.

As I read through this book again after all these years, I realise that this quarter century has been but a short time in history. What I wrote here is still highly relevant.

•

I have made a number of small changes to the wording for this edition. But the story is the same. I have not touched it.

It was not necessary to do so.

HENNING MANKELL

Mozambique, November 1997

THE ROCK BLASTER

The News Item

"Why the hell isn't it going off?"

Norström angrily kicked his left foot. He had got it tangled in a ball of steel wire which someone had carelessly left lying among the rock debris. As he thrashed about, the wire tightened ever higher up his leg. He could easily have bent down and yanked the snarl free with a single tug.

But Norström did not bend down. He kept on furiously kicking. He was sweating. His grey flannel shirt, unbuttoned far down over his bulging stomach, soaked up the sweat and gave off an acrid smell of dirty skin.

Norström was the foreman of a team of detonators. It was a Saturday afternoon in the middle of June and steam was rising from the heat beating down on the unshaded work site. Norström was in charge of blasting tunnels for a railway line. The line was to be made double-track and that required three new tunnels. Right now, they were working on the middle one, also the longest and most awkward. They had just started on the opening in the rock wall. The rough and spiky surface of the grey granite had been laid bare of its thin covering of soil. Sunlight reflected off the cliff face, which rose almost vertically for about thirty metres. There was a hillock, roughly a hundred metres in circumference, and the tunnels and railway line were to go straight through it.

Norström did not like blasting tunnels. "You either get rid of the whole thing or just leave it. Making holes straight through is asking for trouble. Sooner or later it'll collapse." That was his view. In all his fifty years he had been lucky enough not to have to blast tunnels more than once every five years, but now he had three to do in one go.

"Will someone come and get rid of this bloody mess!"

Norström glared angrily at some workers who were resting on their pinch bars. They were gratefully enjoying the unexpected break. First the charge had failed, and then Norström had got his foot tangled up in some steel wire. They leaned on their spikes and waited with their backs turned to the sun.

"You run over and help him."

Oskar Johansson gave the youngest in their team a light kick with the tip of his boot. A lad of fourteen, small and skinny. He leaped up at once and ran across the sandy ground to Norström, quickly bent down and began to tug at the wire.

"Don't pull so bloody hard. Just loosen it."

Norström was becoming more and more annoyed. He squinted at the sun, then turned towards the rock face, glanced down at the boy carefully digging around in the tangle of steel wire, and then glared at the blasters, immobile and leaning on their spikes.

"Why isn't it going off?" he bellowed.

Oskar Johansson straightened up.

"I'll take a look."

At the same time, Norström's foot came free of the wire. The break was over. Now the failed charge had to be checked. And that was Johansson's job, since he had primed it. Every explosion was a personal thing. The dynamite was the same, unpredictable and treacherous, but every charge had its owner, the one responsible for it.

◆

The accelerating pace of industrial expansion made improved communications necessary. The railways had to be extended. There were to be more tracks. There were more and longer trains and the roar of explosions echoed throughout the country.

◆

They were well into summer. The constant heat since the end of May had begun to scorch the ground. When the blasters sought the shade of the birch trees for their short breaks, there was a crackling under their boots.

Johansson wiped his forehead. He looked at the back of his hand. It was shiny with sweat and he wiped it on his shirt. He was twenty-three years old, the youngest in the team of blasters – because the helper did not count. Oskar had already worked on blasting teams for seven years, and enjoyed it. He was tall, well built, with a round face and an open expression which was never serious. His eyes were bright blue, and his fair hair curled over his forehead. The early summer heat had turned his skin brown. He was wearing a grey-white shirt and dark blue cotton trousers, and was barefoot.

He peered towards the rock face.

•

"Will you go and check?"

Norström stood with his hands on his hips and shot Johansson a challenging look. Norström disliked failed detonations. Partly because you never knew what might happen, partly because they held up the work. He was responsible for sticking to the schedule, and he knew this tunnel was going to cause them problems. Besides, he had a hangover. The day before he had turned fifty-five, and there had been a party in the evening. He had drunk akvavit all through the night until he crashed into bed at about two in the morning. And he had vomited at length and copiously when he got up two hours later to go to work. He almost regretted having turned down the offer of a day's holiday to mark his birthday. A gesture from management, in recognition of his having worked for the railway's construction division on and off since 1881. And because he had a reputation for keeping to deadlines and getting work done. This had earned him the nickname "Glory of Labour" from his fellow workers. It was never used in Norström's presence, but that is how he was referred to when the blasters talked about him at home in the evening, or during rest breaks when he was busy with something else. When he first found out that he had a nickname he was angry, but then he began to see it as a sign that the blasters were afraid of him, and he liked that. Now he often used the name to refer to himself, when describing his job to his friends. Only yesterday he had gone on and on about how scared the blasters were of him. He had been with his brother-in-law, who had come to the birthday celebration, and had talked at length about his job.

It was nearly three o'clock, and in three hours their working week would be over. Then they would have a day off and Norström would be able to lie on his bed, swatting at the flies and telling the children to be quiet, and slowly plan next week's work. According to the schedule he had thought out the previous Sunday, they had failed to meet their target. And nothing disturbed him more than when they fell short of expectations. It meant that his Sunday, the rest day, would be ruined. He would spend it fretting.

"Have you pulled off the detonating cable?"

Some of the blasters mumbled an almost inaudible "no".

"Are you out of your minds? Why not?"

Norström was astonished that they had failed to do something so obvious. He had no sympathy for the fact that the blasters had been taking a short break in the heat.

"Get your arse over there now and rip the cable off!"

He gave the helper a kick. The boy quickly scampered over to the small wooden box that stood a short distance from them and tore off a cable which was attached to a steel clip at the back.

Johansson pulled himself up to his full height, propped his metal spike against a huge lump of blast debris and began to walk towards the rock face. He went slowly, as if he did not want to rouse the dynamite. He grimaced in the heat, and wiped the salty sweat from his eyes. A feeling of unease always settled over the entire team whenever an explosive charge did not go off. Dynamite was dangerous. You never knew what tricks it might get up to. But somebody always had to go and check, and caution was the only possible protection.

Johansson stopped just metres short of the rock face. He bit his lower lip and looked carefully at the hole in the cliff into which the detonating cable snaked. He turned around, and in a low voice called over to the others still standing there leaning on their spikes:

"Is the cable off?"

Norström strode over to the wooden box himself, something he did not usually do, had a look and then shouted:

"It's disconnected. You can go on over."

Johansson nodded, more for his own benefit than Norström's. He did it to convince himself that everything was ready.

◆

Then he turns, fixes his eyes on the drill-hole and slowly approaches the rock wall with short, stealthy steps. He does not take his eyes off the hole. He bites his lip, sweat pouring down his face, he blinks to clear his vision and when he is half a metre from the cliff he stops and carefully leans forward. Without relaxing his concentration, he slowly stretches out his right arm until his hand is resting just above the hole. He focuses, braces himself and begins to tease out the detonating cable. He hears the faint sound of a metal spike clinking as it is laid against a stone. His fingertips tighten around the cable.

The next moment the rock wall explodes, and for many years afterwards foreman Norström will tell people how it was one of his men who, while working on the middle one of three railway tunnels, astonishingly survived an explosion at close range. His name was Oskar Johansson, and their helper, a lad of just fourteen years, fainted when they found Johansson's right hand, rotting in a bush seventy metres away. They found it thanks to the flies that had gathered around. It was lying among the dandelions, its fingers stretched out.

And Norström would add that Johansson not only survived but kept on working as a blaster once he had recovered.

◆

That Saturday afternoon in June 1911, Oskar Johansson lost all his fair hair. His left eye was ripped out of its socket by the force of the blast. The right hand was severed at the wrist by a shard of rock. It was sliced off with an almost surgical precision. Another shard tore through Oskar's lower abdomen like a red-hot arrow, severed half of his penis on the way through and emerged via his groin, kidney and bladder.

But Oskar Johansson survived, carried on working as a rock blaster until his retirement, and did not die until April 9, 1969.

◆

On the following Monday, the local newspapers reported that a young rock blaster had died in a terrible and harrowing accident. Nobody had been able to prevent the tragedy. The incident was attributable to the dangers of dynamite. By a small mercy nobody else was hurt, and the deceased did not have any family which would now be left destitute.

◆

The story was never corrected.

1962

The alarm clock rings, shrill and merciless. It is a quarter past three in the morning in the middle of May. The oil-fired heater is cold and the room chilly and damp. The sea, blue-black and still. A heavy grey-white mist weighs on the surface of the water. Barren images moulded by the leaden light. Oak branches rising like ruins out of the grey haze.

As I walk along the path that hugs the shoreline, the sand and the brown-grey seaweed crunch like eggshells under my heels. A gentle ripple crosses the water. Dying waves roll soundlessly past. Somewhere in the distance, a boat has been sailing by. A pike splashes on the surface and the sound bounces back and forth between the cliffs on the far side of the inlet.

The island is not big. It takes half an hour to walk around it. To the headland, where Johansson has his cabin, it's about fifteen minutes. I follow the shore, branch off in among the oaks where the sand gives way to steep boulders, get back down to the beach again, squeeze my way through a tight thicket of alder and then I only have to follow the gentle curve of the cove along to the headland, where the house is.

The door is ajar. Oskar is already up. He is sitting at the table playing Patience, a very special version of Idiot's

Delight. He nods at me and I pick up the coffee pot standing on the spirit stove. I sit down on the bench, help myself to a blue-speckled cup and then I just wait until Johansson says it is time to go.

◆

Oskar bought his cabin, an old sauna, seven years ago. It was at the time when the military were disposing of the remaining barracks buildings from the emergency standby years of the Second World War. Oskar was able to buy the bathhouse for 150 kronor, provided he removed the building himself. But Oskar talked to the owner of the land on which it stood and was given permission to leave the sauna there and to occupy it for as long as he lived. The following year I helped him to tear out the benches, line the walls with hardwood, make a small partition for his bed, fit a cupboard and open up a window. Then we painted the whole thing white and red. Johansson moves out to the island at the beginning of April and stays there until it turns cold in October.

◆

The sauna is one and a half metres wide and little more than three metres long. When I stand on tiptoe, my head touches the ceiling.

The bed: the creaky old officer's bed which he was given for free when the large barracks building up on the slope was torn down.

A brown blanket, two changes of sheets, pillowcases with the red border and the initials A. J. in ornate letters. Two brown kitchen chairs, the lath table with the green wax table-cloth. Spirit stove, paraffin lamp, transistor radio, pack of cards, spectacles, wallet.

The cups, the plates, the coffee and the potatoes.

◆

With the index finger of his left hand, Johansson presses a button on the radio. The finger is thick, stronger than two normal ones. All he has left on that hand is the thumb and this index finger, and together they have developed into a claw for gripping things which has had to assume the functions of both hands. The index finger presses down and music fills the room, much too loudly. But it is a sign. Soon we will get up and go. Just before half past four we sit in Johansson's rowing boat. It is light, made of hardboard riveted to a simple wooden frame. Grass-green and flat-bottomed. I sit in the stern and Johansson rows out from the shore. He grips the left oar with his finger and thumb. The right one is firmly in the crook of his right arm. Once we have cleared the three wooden planks that make up Johansson's jetty, he turns the boat and we glide over towards the other side of the headland.

We move across the water in silence. It is still chilly and the mist as grey as before. Johansson's oar strokes are steady and follow the rhythm of his breathing. When he pauses, he also holds his breath.

Our nets are on the other side of the promontory. One for perch. One for flounder. First the perch. Then the flounder. We pull the nets up in the same order as we always do.

With me crouching in the stern. Johansson slowly rowing the boat backwards. Every fish we get is counted out loud by Johansson. A number, then another number. Just that.

"One."

"Two."

"Three."

"Four."

One big perch and three flounder. They flap about between our feet in the bottom of the boat. The nets in a pile over my boots. Johansson turns the boat around and we row back.

◆

May 1962. We are listening to Radio Nord. Johansson usually laughs when the voice on the radio announces the transmission frequency and talks about megacycles.

"What the hell are they doing? Cycling around on the boat...?"

He chuckles to himself and squints at me with his one eye. His index finger is drumming on the wax tablecloth.

◆

The fog is still just as thick, the sea equally leaden, but the light is growing brighter and cutting through the haze. Johansson twists around in his chair, grips the back of it with his finger and thumb and drags himself to his feet, enough to be able to see out through the window. He has a quick look and sinks back onto his chair again, and returns to his special version of Idiot's Delight.

The cards are dirty and coming apart. The Jack of Spades has a bloodstain on one of his faces. The Seven of Clubs is from a different pack. One has all sorts of sailing boats on the back. The other a dark red background with a thin white border.

◆

Radio Nord is playing "The Last of the Mohicans" by Little Gerhard.

◆

The index finger drums slowly on the tablecloth, like a dripping icicle. The Idiot's Delight will not work out.

1911

"I'd met her half a year before the accident. Pretty much exactly half a year. We got serious in June. We hadn't really talked much about getting married. But in those days, there was no question of anything else. If you met and started walking out then you were supposed to marry. She was the same age as me. There were three days between us, she was just those few days older. We used to meet on Thursday evenings. The only time she could manage. She had four hours off then. She worked for the manager of a textile company, looking after his small children. A boy and twin girls. She slept in a room at the back of the nursery. She belonged to that generation of working-class girls who spent most of their youth with a middle-class family, tucked away either behind a kitchen or in the children's room. She didn't like children at all, but that was the only work she could find. Mostly we used to walk around town. I don't really remember what we talked about nor what we looked at. We just walked."

◆

"But there's one thing I do recall. It must have been about a month before the accident. It was graduation day at the town's high school. A Thursday, and we were out walking. Then three of those students came towards us on the pavement and refused to make way, so she and I were both jostled. I remember it clearly. It's usually those sorts of things that come back to me. Meaningless details like that."

◆

Elly comes out of the kitchen entrance. She is wearing a white dress, brown boots and a black shawl over her shoulders. She is quite short, a little chubby. Round face. Fresh complexion and green eyes. Brown frizzy hair. Pinched lips. Her teeth are pale yellow and she has already lost one, in her upper jaw, just where her laugh usually ends.

Johansson is waiting outside the iron gate. He watches Elly walking down the broad gravel path which leads from the white three-storey house. She gives an embarrassed little smile as she fumbles with the lock on the inside of the gate. Then they stand there, face to face, nod and start walking along the pavement. They don't talk. The air is warm. They go along a street with high iron railings on each side, high walls, white detached houses. They head for the centre of town, towards their own world.

"How's it looking for you next Thursday?" Oskar asks Elly.

Elly answers. "I'm probably free then too."

An orange tram clanks past on its way into town. They pause and look to see whether there are any familiar faces in the two carriages. They stand and watch it make a stop, a middle-aged couple get off and stroll towards Oskar and Elly. A soft wind is blowing. Elly brushes her face with her hand, looks away from Oskar when she smiles. Oskar takes her hand. He has washed himself with special care today, as he does every Thursday.

A month from now his hand will be lying with outstretched fingers among dandelions, while the blasting crew stand looking at it with numb faces.

Oskar and Elly cut across the cobbled square. In the distance, three students are approaching.

◆

"Latin was the worst. Enoksson's never liked me. He'd have flunked me, given half a chance."

Black patent-leather shoes, blue walking sticks with silver-grey tips. Quick, jerky steps over the cobbles. A black-clad foot which changes direction in mid-air, narrowly avoiding a brown, sticky heap of excrement.

"Just imagine, they failed seven people this year. Many of the classes were weak."

"That's those plebs."

Patent-leather shoes, clattering footsteps.

"Now look at that. See the girl over there. In the white dress. She's one of our maids. Got big breasts. I'm going to walk in on her one evening and grab a handful."

"How much will you pay her?"

"Ten kronor, but then it's the whole hog."

"Have you done it before?"

"Of course. Twice."

"With her?"

"With prettier ones."

"Who's she with?"

"Don't know."

"Shall we push them around a bit?"

"Yes, let's."

Patent-leather shoes, pointed ones. Silk socks. Grey woollen trousers. Jackets. The white student's cap. Spots on their chins, their backs, their buttocks. Elbows that have not yet been sharpened jab Oskar and Elly in the side. A greeting, cigar out of the mouth, cap in slim hand.

"Good evening, Elly."

◆

Oskar says nothing. They walk on and he holds on to her hand. But then, trying to make it sound unimportant, he quickly asks:

"Did you know them?"

And Elly. Elly, you cannot leave this unanswered.

"He's a son in the house where I work. From another marriage."

"I see."

Oskar's face darkens. He slams his heels into the cobblestones. With jealousy welling up, he can feel an evil thought gnawing all the way down to the pit of his stomach.

"Fucking bastard. Did he shove you too?"

"A bit."

Oskar looks like thunder. Fucking rock blaster, working-class pig, nothing but riff-raff. Twelve children in a kitchen, another ten in the living room. Stack them up on top of each other. Rat-catchers. Mouldy food. Let them freeze. Block out the sun with tall white houses. Build our houses, and walls to shut out the sun. Pull their teeth, remove their vocal chords. Bang nails through their feet.

"What is it, Oskar?"

Elly pulls her hand away. She looks at him. He shakes his head.

"Nothing. I was just thinking."

One more block to go. The sun's setting.

"What were you thinking about?"

One more block.

"Nothing in particular. Shall we turn back?"

"Might as well."

And already they have turned around. Piano music can be heard from an open window. Elly and Oskar. Elly and Oskar.

◆

The town they have to cross: wooden hovels clinging desperately to one another, propping each other up, warming each other. High white brick walls framing a square, screening off the slums. The short walk from the middle-class homes. The long way back.

◆

Elly goes into her room beyond the nursery. The other girl is already asleep. Her blanket has slipped off. She is snoring, open-mouthed. The noise cuts into Elly's ears. She takes off her white dress. Without knowing why, she pushes it under her end of the long, narrow pillow. Clambers over her bedfellow and lies down against the wall. Slowly, she runs her little fingernail along the wallpaper. She thinks she can see a tram in the white-brown pattern. She falls asleep with that image in her mind.

◆

As to Elly: in the spring of 1911 she is twenty-three years old. Her employer is the manager of a textile company in the town.

As to Oskar: he is wandering through the streets. In seven hours, he will be standing in front of Norström, holding his metal spike in his hand.

The Island

The fog has lifted. I get up to go. Oskar is shuffling his cards. He uses his thumb to lay them out in a row along the table. He stirs them around with his index finger. With his thumb he pushes them together again into a stack.

"Shall we put them out tonight?"

"Yes. We should get more tomorrow."

"I'll be along at about seven. 'Bye till then."

"'Bye."

Oskar is sitting on the chair. It is a quarter past seven. Soon he will lie down on his bed. Soon he will sleep for a few hours.

◆

The island is in the outer archipelago. It is shaped like a truncated boomerang. There are oaks, birches, cliffs and sand. From three sides you can look straight out to the open sea. The fourth side slopes down into a narrow strait which leads to an island with a fishing village.

On a national survey map, the island is shown as a nameless rocky islet.

The customs boat ties up at the island once in the spring, once in the autumn. There is a radio antenna on the highest point. The customs officers usually come down to Johansson's old sauna to say hello. You can hear Radio Nord blaring out across the water. The customs men laugh, and so does Oskar. One of them goes around to the back of the cabin. There is a food store there, dug into the ground. A square one metre deep, with a wooden cover. They fetch out the cans of beer, go back into the cabin, and every now and then you hear the sound of Oskar's rough voice shouting out.

The Sisters

"It's a bit strange, I suppose, that I ended up marrying her sister. But it took over a year for me to recover and Elly moved away. At first, she used to come and visit me, but I could tell that seeing my injuries was painful for her. I think the eye bothered her less than my hand. Then she just told me that she was leaving town, and she did look rather fat, although she tried to hide it. I don't remember feeling all that much. I'd had all my pain. I knew her sister for nearly three months before I realised that she was Elly's younger sister. It wasn't as if they were alike. The colour of their hair perhaps, but nothing else. I saw Elly several times after we got married. There were never any problems. She had a good man. And we had never really got that close. I read in the paper a few years ago that Elly had died."

The Oar Strokes

Oskar moves his oars in time with his breathing.

His many voices form a whole which does not actually exist.

◆

Oskar is distorting his own history. He claims a poor memory, that none of it is important, that he does not feel like talking about it. He picks fragments out of his story and gives a terse account of them, while drumming his index finger on the wax tablecloth. Rarely answers questions. Doesn't avoid them, but his replies are always ambiguous and open-ended.

◆

His way of being evasive.

◆

"Others have already described it so well."

"I don't really remember that bit."

◆

Surely you can't have forgotten.

◆

We are sitting on the bench outside the sauna. Hitting out at flies, mending nets, drinking coffee, and occasionally Oskar mentions something in passing. I hear the words, close up the gaps between them, fill in the margins.

◆

Oskar Johansson, the rock blaster with the damaged body. He is there, and he mentions something in passing. His sentences weave in and out.

◆

The alarm clock keeps ringing, harsh and unrelenting, and the sauna is always the same distance away.

◆

We sit in the rowing boat.
    Oskar's flat tone as he counts the fish we catch.

◆

The playing cards, Radio Nord, frequencies and blue-speckled cups.

◆

And the narrator?
    Oskar thinks he is too slow at pulling up the nets.

Oskar Johansson

Oskar was born in Norrköping in 1888. He was the third of five children. Three sisters and two brothers. Elsa, Karl, Oskar, Anna, Viktoria. Elsa and Viktoria died young. He never saw Elsa. By the time Oskar was born, she was no longer even a sad memory. When Oskar was seven, his father came out into the backyard one day looking serious, took Oskar gently by the arm and told him to come indoors. His mother was sitting in the kitchen crying, and his father told Oskar that Viktoria had fallen down the steep drop behind the houses and that she was dead. So Oskar had to stay indoors for a while and be sad.

Later they stood around the little hole in the graveyard and his father tried to comfort his mother by saying that they did not need any more children. Three were enough.

◆

"I don't really remember so much of all that. What we used to do. There was nothing special about me. I played the same games as all other children. Had the same clothes. Sometimes they were whole, sometimes torn. We played in the backyards. Running around and shouting at each other. We chased cats when we found them. We pushed one into a hole under the privy in the yard one day and blocked it up with pieces of wood. It was white. I think it was called Putte. And I ran to school like everybody else. There was nothing unusual. Sometimes I ask myself what I thought of back in those days. It might be fun to remember. But I don't. I suppose most of the time I just ran around and screamed along with the rest of them. We clambered out over the planks, climbed back in again, went home quickly to get some food, and then charged around the backyards. There were four or so of us boys who stuck together. One was called Oskar, like me. We pretended to be brothers. His father ended up hanging himself and I think his mother went and did the same thing a few years later. But there was never anything special about me. I played like all the others. The same games."

◆

One day, in the third summer, there is someone sitting next to Oskar outside the sauna. When I arrive, he nods.

"I'm Karl."

Oskar gives a little smile.

"He's my brother."

"We haven't seen each other for a long time."

Then they sit on the wooden bench and look out over the water and talk. Karl is only there for the day. A boat comes to fetch him. He has to go back to an old people's home somewhere. The brothers shake hands, Karl walks carefully out along the planks, climbs into the boat, which reverses out, turns around and disappears behind the headland.

The Accident

Once the rumble had died down and the first shock subsided, Norström half-ran up to the rock wall ahead of the others.

"You stay right where you are. I don't want you to see this."

Norström yelled at the young helper not to move. He was standing among the scattered metal spikes. He was shaking all over and tears welled up in his eyes.

"Christ, that's horrible."

The blasting crew stood in a semicircle a few metres back from Oskar, who was lying twisted on the ground with blood pouring, pumping out from various parts of his body. His fair hair has been scorched off and there is a smell of burnt skin. The monotone buzzing of the blow-flies cuts into their ears.

Then, suddenly, Oskar's right leg twitches.

"What the fuck. He's alive."

"What?"

"He's alive."

"How the hell . . ."

"Off with your shirts. Bandage him every bloody where. Quick."

The blasters tear off their shirts. They stop up the bleeding holes as best they can, the mutilated body parts. Norström bellows.

"Run like fuck and get a cart. Oskar's alive."

And the young helper runs.

◆

And there is no time to wait for anything else. Oskar's body is lying there on a cart and the blasters rush towards town, through the streets in the direction of the hospital. They hurtle along with their cart rattling and bouncing over the cobblestones. People stop on the pavements, turn, shout out "What's happened?", but get no answer. Up the gravel path to the hospital, Norström charges in through the doors, on the verge of exhaustion, his heart pumping wildly.

"Quick, quick!"

Once the white coats have realised what has occurred and that there is still life in the body on the wooden cart, everything happens very rapidly. Caring hands lift the body, charred and covered in red blotches, lay it on a stretcher and vanish through doors, down corridors.

◆

What about the rock blasters, drained as they were, what did they do? Sit down in the sun on the steps, shaken and scared? Or did they go back? Or go off in different directions?

◆

One day I did get an answer, without asking.

"Even though I worked with pretty much the same blokes for a number of years, I don't remember a single name. Norström, of course, but none of the others. That's how it was.

We were so anonymous to everyone else. We had no value other than as blasters. A bunch of blasters, a bunch of carpenters, a bunch of textile workers. We even saw ourselves as a bunch of blasters. A sort of self-contempt, I suppose. Sometimes they would come up to the hospital. Norström visited me and said he was proud that I had made it. Nobody in any other team of blasters he knew of had survived a bang like that. The other men just sat there in silence, maybe asked how I was. If they told me anything at all, then it was that they'd actually kept working for another hour that day after running to the hospital."

◆

"They had cleaned up after the blast. But they didn't find my right hand until the Monday. Basically we were just a bunch of blasters. If anyone had a name it was a nickname."

◆

But this is where Oskar is wrong. Here, he himself will change his story. His memory is split. Oskar was a different person then. Now his account is elusive. Not because there is anything he wants to hide, but because he thinks it does not matter.

◆

Oskar Johansson has been a worker all his life. His thoughts and actions have changed, yet all along he has been a worker. What changed his thinking? What changed the things he has done? Why does he talk of bunches of blasters, bunches of carpenters?

Oskar is sixty-eight when we first meet. He has been living in his apartment in town together with his wife, Elly's sister. Then she dies and he stays there on his own and comes out here in the summer. Usually it is his eldest, his son, who drives him down to the boat harbour and fetches him home in the autumn. The son has his own company. He owns a laundry business. Oskar and Elly's sister have two more children. Both girls. They are married and live elsewhere in the country. Oskar also has grandchildren, through his son as well as his daughters.

Oskar's place in town is a two-roomed apartment in a rental block built in the late forties. It is on the ground floor, in a neighbourhood that is just being redeveloped. I don't recall if it is entrance A, B or C, but the building is still there. Inside one of the ground floor windows there are heavy, flourishing pot plants. Maybe that was where he lived. I could ask, but it is unimportant.

◆

Oskar is a special and rare case. A worker who has survived an explosion at close range. That is why he has a room of his own. It has a high ceiling. Since Oskar is going to be there for a long time, they hang a portrait of the royal family on the wall opposite the bed. The king and queen are seated, the princes and princesses, the brothers-in-law and cousins stand. Wishy-washy pale colours. Oskar's room is on the top floor. He can see the sky and the outline of tin roofs right at the bottom of the window. Sometimes a pigeon flutters into view. Sometimes two or ten of them.

"Most of the time I would just be lying there on my back, looking out of the window. There was nothing to see. But I probably just lay there waiting for something to turn up outside. They couldn't do much about the pain, of course. After about half a year something did in fact show up. It was a yellow hot air balloon with a basket under it. It drifted by the window. It was far away, so I was able to watch it for a long time. There were a few people in the basket. Looking in different directions. There may have been some sort of race going on and they had got lost, were off course.

"You can't ever really bear the pain, but you can get used to it. I remember my eye being the worst. It didn't actually hurt, but I had this strange feeling in the empty socket where the eye had been. I kept wanting to blink, but there was nothing there. I remember quite well what I was thinking at the time. Probably because I had nothing to do."

◆

Oskar's case has been carefully documented by both blasting experts and doctors. There are sketches and X-rays, photographs. There are the succinct notes in his medical records. There is Norström's extravagant account of what happened that Saturday afternoon shortly after three o'clock. There are Oskar's own words. A few simple sentences. Short, hesitant.

"I had just got hold of the detonating cable. I was about to start pulling. Then there was a kind of flash."

◆

Oskar's case was inexplicable. The blasting experts suggested electric impulses, overheating. The doctors talked about unaccountably light injuries. But the case was diagnosed as "ultimately impossible to explain completely".

◆

A university professor visited Oskar several times during the autumn. He was a theologian.

"Like everybody else, he asked if I remembered anything. But I didn't. They wanted to know if everything had suddenly gone black and I said it had gone white. They asked when I had come to again and I told them I didn't remember. But they never believed me. Why would I hide anything? It was just that I couldn't remember."

The medical records are written in a spindly hand that is hard to read. They have been kept.

For whom?

◆

After a heavy shower in August, Oskar notices that water is dripping in through the corner just above the spirit stove. I take a quick look and see that the roofing felt is rotting there.

"We'll have to re-line the whole roof. Might as well do it, if I'm going to go on living."

◆

The mail boat brings out the felt. As I lie on the roof hammering in nails, I hear Radio Nord coming from the room below.

Sometimes there is the sound of shuffling across the floor. Ten minutes later, the coffee is ready.

Boiled coffee, on the weak side.

The last summer Oskar visited the island he returned to his apartment on October 24. A strong north wind was blowing, making it difficult for the boat that came to fetch him to come in by the planks that made up Johansson's jetty.

In the middle of November, one of his legs began to feel bad. In the mornings it was almost dead, without any sensation. He went to the hospital and was admitted for the second time in his life. This would be the last time. He got gangrene in his leg. It was amputated and one morning just before Christmas he had a brain haemorrhage. His other leg became paralysed, and one of his arms, and he could no longer speak. He remained like that until the beginning of April. Then he had another stroke and died an hour past midnight on April 9.

It was a Tuesday. The funeral was on the Saturday. At 12.45 the bells began to toll, and the congregation consisted of his children. The coffin was brown. Real candles and a simple floral arrangement, which the undertakers had organised. Two short organ pieces, the priest reading from the service handbook and the ceremony is over. Outside, the air is sharp. Work is being done on the flower beds in the churchyard. The siblings go off together to have coffee, agree on a day to settle the estate.

On the Monday the death is announced in the only remaining local newspaper.

The funeral has taken place.

The urn with the ashes is interred a month later. Oskar's son drives to the churchyard during his lunch break.

◆

It does not take long to settle the estate. No-one wants the furniture. Linen, household equipment, books, pictures and the television are divided without difficulty. The small amount of money will pay for the funeral. The clothes are burned.

Nobody ever came to take away any of the things that Oskar had left in the cabin. The radio is still there, an old tin pillbox with a few 10-öre coins in it, some sheets and pillowcases. Mirror, saucepan and cracked blue cups.

◆

The smell is still there. The bitter smell of old age.

The Key Words

This story.

Tiny beads of narrative that string together to form a rosary.

◆

The notes and the memories. The two Oskar Johanssons. One a genuine former rock blaster who spent his summers living in an old sauna. The other an Oskar Johansson who becomes a part of a story. But both of them died one day, of a brain haemorrhage.

◆

This account is an attempt to piece together what Oskar never actually said. To try to describe what caused the changes in him.

◆

There are a few key words.

◆

"I played the same games as all the others."

"I obviously went on working as a blaster, as soon as I'd recovered."

"I've been a worker all my life."

"Lots of things have changed, but not for us."

Elly

A lamp on the bedside table casts a faint, pale light through its shade. Oskar is lying on his back in bed and his breathing is regular. His head is wrapped in white bandages. A thick wad of dressing is held in place over his left eye by a strip of gauze tied around his jaw and the top of his head. The blue-white blanket has been drawn up to his chin. What one can see of Oskar's face, his mouth, the right eye – which is closed – one cheek, his nose, is pallid yellow. His arms are resting on top of the blanket. The right one ends in a bundle of gauze and compresses. There is a similar round white shape over his left hand. The bed-cover is raised over the pelvis and lower abdomen because of all the bulky bandages dressing the wounds ripped open by the dynamite.

Oskar's bed is grey-blue. The paint has peeled in some places and the steel shows through. His medical notes are hanging at the foot of the bed. The temperature chart sketches the contours of an Alpine landscape which gradually evens out into unbroken terrain. The curtains are closed. Everything in the room is stiff and pale.

A white-haired night nurse opens the door. She tiptoes up to the bed, leans over Oskar, listens, puts one hand on his heart. Then she turns, pads out and shuts the door.

Oskar is not sleeping. He lies there, listening to his pain. Under the bandage over his eye, there is a twitch in the empty socket. He tries to picture the hole, but the image jumps about, jerky, unsteady. One moment all he sees is a red hole, then it changes to a slimy lump of pus floating about in a bowl of skin. The eye is gone, but the spasms remain, echoes of the blinking that is no longer there. The constant reminder makes him feel faintly, persistently sick. Oskar tries to focus his thoughts and mental images on other things, but every third second his eye blinks and the empty left socket responds.

A constant pain pierces his abdomen. It throbs and sears through all his shredded nerves. Oskar does not know exactly what has happened, other than that half his penis has been torn off, but that the urethra and the scrotum with the testicles are intact. He does not know, has not seen. It is all wrapped up in a thick bundle, but he can feel the mess and the stickiness underneath. Each time the bandages are changed, he tries to steel himself to look, but he either cannot or does not want to. Every movement, every twisting of his body, causes unbearable pain and he cries out. At first, he tried with all his might not to. He bit holes in his tongue, tensed every undamaged muscle in his body to strain against the scream bubbling up in his chest, but he could never stop it from bursting out. Now he does not even try to resist.

Oskar dozes off at regular intervals. There is no difference between night and day. Five times in every twenty-four hours he is given liquid sustenance, a warm hand supports the back of his neck and each sip sets fire to his torment. When he urinates, the bandages are changed. Then he sleeps, wakes up when he moves, lies and looks or shuts his eye and day is the same as night. The hours flow together and thoughts and images flit through his mind.

To Oskar, none of this is real. Everything is only strange and he is unable to grasp what has happened even when his mind is least affected by the drugs. It is beyond his comprehension. He sees no images of a cliffside exploding. No images of himself in the June heat, watching from a distance as he stands by a rock wall, gripping a detonating cable with one hand and then being blown into nothingness. No images that show him lying on the ground, contorted. There is no sound of Norström bellowing or the young helper crying. An endless row of people dressed in white glides through Oskar's mind. Dressed in white, but with bright faces, they sometimes take on Elly's appearance. Faces that look down at him, smile at him, stroke his cheek, straighten out his blanket, change his bandages. Reality is reduced to what is immediately present. Everything else is gone. There are no memories staring at him from within his head. There is no inkling of anything from his past. His world is reduced to what is palpable, easily grasped. It is confined within these walls. Infinity is the blue or grey sky. He travels when his bed is pushed through the corridors to X-ray and the laboratories. The faces looking down at him in his bed represent both event and memory all at once.

The only thing that remains from another time is Elly's face. She has not yet been allowed to visit him. He is not well enough. But there is her face, leaning over him and smiling her pinched smile. During the day her face sometimes appears outside the window, in relief against the grey or blue background.

And then there are the dreams. Vividly coloured and chaotic. Since he wakes up so often, he nearly always recalls them. Every new waking spell begins with him looking back at the most recent dream.

There is one where he is sitting in a dark cellar sewing flags. A narrow slit of a window, just where the wall meets the roof, lets a faint light into the room. The walls are grey, bare. The floor is of trodden clay. The air is cold and damp. He is sitting on a brown wooden table in the middle of the room, sewing hems on flags that are two metres long. A roll of yellow-and-blue material is standing by one of the walls. The yellow cross is already woven into the coarse cloth. He sits and sews, pushing the needle up and down through the hem, with the thread winding into an even spiral. And then the flag in his lap begins to flutter. A wind starts blowing in the room and the fabric slaps against his knees. The only sounds are those of the flag beating against his legs.

In another dream, Elly and he are running along a street at night, chasing an enormous rat which is galloping ahead of them. It is the size of an Alsatian. There are mouldy spots all over its brown coat. Its grey tail whips against the paving stones like a length of steel wire. Elly and he run after the rat. Suddenly he sees that Elly is also a rat, with tiny dark brown eyes.

He wakes up and runs the images of his dreams through his mind once more. For him they are pictures, two-dimensional. Nothing more. He opens his eye, the empty socket twitches under the bandage and he sees the portrait of the royal family on the wall opposite.

Day is dawning. The steely light of early morning. Soft sounds from the corridor outside his door make their way into the room. Footsteps, voices growing louder and then moving on.

Oskar has been in hospital for two months and ten days. Outside, summer is coming to an end and the blasters have just started on the third and last railway tunnel.

This breaking day is different for Oskar. He is going to have visitors, although he does not know it. Elly is coming. Norström is coming. And through their words Oskar will begin to understand what has actually happened. His mind will turn to wondering, the images and the dreams will be different.

◆

It is afternoon, and Norström is the first to arrive. He enters the room. He has changed out of his work clothes and is wearing a black suit which is too small for him. His collar feels tight and he is afraid and sweaty-faced. He is twisting his mouth round and round and trying to wet his lips. He pulls up a chair and drops heavily onto it. Sits and looks at Oskar.

"Well then, Johansson. You made it. Not bad, bloody good effort. We thought you were done for. Hard to imagine anything else. The thing went off only half a metre from you. Damn near brought down the whole rock face."

He wipes his lips and tries to hide the mixture of disgust

and unease he feels at the sight of Oskar lying there, wrapped in bandages and blankets.

"Must hurt like hell, I suppose. It seemed pretty bad when we got to you."

Oskar looks with his one eye. He recognises Norström, but he does not understand what he is hearing and cannot place it in any context.

"I won't stay for long. They said you had another visitor."

Norström tries to look cheerful. He feels uncomfortable and wants to get away even after just these few minutes. His mouth is dry and his lips move faster and faster. He tries to suck on his teeth to get the saliva going.

"We'll do our best to come along quite often now, one of the boys or I. We weren't allowed to before."

Silence. Oskar tries to smile, but the bandages are tugging.

"Well. I'd better be going, then."

Norström gets up, wonders if he should move the chair back, but he leaves it where it is.

"Fine. 'Bye then. You get better now."

Norström walks towards the door, turns around and looks once more at Oskar. Then he goes out and gently closes the door.

◆

Something is troubling Oskar. An obscure memory is starting to nag at his consciousness. But as yet he does not know what it is.

◆

Elly.

She is sitting on the edge of the bed, staring at you.

Was it really that awful?

It must hurt so much.

Isn't there anything left of the eye?

◆

Oskar.

She sits on the edge of the bed. I recognise that dress.

I don't remember.

I've got used to it.

Apparently there's nothing left.

◆

Elly. Tell me what happened.

◆

"I saw in the paper on the Monday that you were dead. It had fallen onto the floor from the table in the hall. I was just going to put it back. I was on my way to the kitchen to have my morning coffee."

Now she is crying. Floods of tears as she leans down towards Oskar who is lying in the bed with his blanket pulled up to his chin.

"It was so awful. I thought I was going to faint. I had to sit down on the floor. I sat on top of the galoshes and was shaking all over. My heart kept beating faster. I thought I was going to die. Then I went straight in to the lady of the house and said that my husband had been killed in an accident and that I couldn't work. That's what I said. My husband is dead, and the lady sat there on the little sofa eating her breakfast and got cross because I hadn't knocked."

"But you're not married, Elly. Not as far as I know. Now go back to the nursery. I don't want the children to be left alone. Go back now."

"But my husband is dead. It says so in the paper."

Elly is standing there holding the newspaper. She takes the remaining steps to the sofa where the lady is sitting with her tea, and holds up the newspaper. With both hands.

"It says so here."

And the lady of the house takes it, reads the piece.

"But surely your name isn't Johansson? It's Lundgren. If Johansson is a close friend of yours then I understand that it's sad. But go back to the nursery now. Someone must be with the children. Take them out this afternoon. They need it. It's nice and warm. Go now. Leave the newspaper here."

And she goes back to her breakfast and Elly leaves the room.

"Close the door, Elly."

Elly closes the door. Elly goes into her room and lies down on her bed. She curls up into the foetal position and tightens every muscle in her body. She moves slowly. She rocks back and forth.

But the accident, Elly?

What do you mean?

I don't know anything about it.

◆

Elly sits on the edge of the bed. She is wearing her white dress.

"I heard there was an explosion. They pulled you through town on a cart. Nobody thought you had survived. Nobody thought you would live. The paper said you were dead."

And suddenly there you are, Oskar, standing by the rock wall one afternoon in June and pulling at a length of detonating cable winding into a drill hole. Then what? Your eye wanders from Elly's face to the royal family on the wall. And you see yourself. Standing up the slope, a short distance from the excavation site. You see yourself standing by the rock wall and suddenly the whole thing explodes and you're thrown backwards and end up as a mutilated body lying in the gravel.

◆

Elly puts her hand on the blanket. Her touch is light, you hardly feel it.

"Was that how it was? Is that what happened?"

"Yes."

"An accident?"

"Yes."

◆

That's why I'm lying here. I was in a blasting accident. A charge that tricked you. Dynamite that shot out of the rock with furious force and tore you to pieces.

◆

Elly.

"I'm so glad you're alive, Oskar."

Elly's visits.

At first every day. Then every third. Then once a week.

Then one last time.

◆

Elly in a white dress. She is standing by your bed. Looking down at her clasped hands.

"What is it, Elly?"

"I've met someone else. We're leaving town."

And you notice that her stomach is a bit rounded. But what are you thinking? What are you feeling?

"I don't remember. It must have been hard. It was unexpected. Because when she came to visit me the week before she hadn't mentioned anything. And she wasn't behaving in a funny way either. I was probably trying to pretend it wasn't happening. But it's easy to understand. I must have looked dreadful. After all, in those days you needed strong hands and healthy men. And she did get a good one too. When she died a few years ago I saw in the death announcement that there were many children and grandchildren. One of them was called Oskar, I remember."

Oskar Johannes Johansson

Oskar sits on the chair. His index finger drumming. It is evening and we are waiting for the rain to stop. The light in the sauna is fading. The paraffin lamp is lit. We are not going to put out any nets. It is too late for that. But on many evenings we just sit and wait for it to stop raining. If it goes on all night then Oskar stays up. He never sleeps when it rains.

"I find it hard to go to sleep."

◆

August. The summer visitors are beginning to desert the archipelago. Fewer boats pass the island. The only ones left are the permanent residents. This morning, when we took up the nets, we saw a solitary sailing boat disappearing out to sea.

◆

Elly goes. She is glad that Oskar is going to live. She promises to write. Her hand brushes the blanket. Then she is gone.

And Oskar is there in his bed with his head saying no, no. He can't help it that his eye begins to run. And the empty socket responds.

◆

The other visitors.

The theologian.

Norström.

The other blasters.

But his parents? His sister and brother?

◆

The third summer he talks about it.

"My father and I had fallen out. He must have been fifty plus and was tired and worn out. He used to empty waste from privies and it was heavy work. There were three of them dealing with a huge number of houses and they had to slave away night and day. Sometimes he said that he was worse off than everybody else. A shit collector, that's what I am. All year round. He never had any time off, and was never rid of the smell. I can't ever remember him laughing. He sometimes smiled, but that only made him look sad. In any case, we had a row. It was about the agitator. There was to be a meeting at another estate nearby and I was going. It wasn't that man Palm. It was somebody less well known. He was both an auctioneer and an agitator, from Blekinge, and he had this funny dialect. But he spoke well and we were all stirred up by the time the meeting ended. I bought a paper off him for fifty öre and when I came home with it and put it on the kitchen table and Far saw it, he became angry. He grabbed it, stared at a picture of the king on the front page, and then he saw that there was a drawing underneath so that it looked as if the king was standing on the head of someone who was supposed to be a dock worker or something like that. At that, he said that he did not want to see this in his house. It would only cause even more misery. Then he stared at me and asked if I was one of those. And I said yes, mostly just to be cheeky, I suppose."

"What did he look like, your Pappa?"

"Hard to say. More than anything else he was tired."

◆

A spring day in 1910. A conversation.

"Can't this be banned? They're so easily influenced."

"I don't think so. They'll rage for a while. Then things will calm down."

"Wouldn't it be best if it was forbidden?"

"Of course. But you can't, except by threatening them. The owner of the property has given his permission."

"Who is he?"

"I don't remember the name. But it's the brewer."

"Kvist?"

"That's the one."

"What do they hope to gain by this? Do the workers really understand what they're being told?"

"Some of them maybe. But it's a language of one and one makes two and no frills."

"What's the subject of the meeting?"

"A hey and a ho for the revolution . . ."

Laughter. Drawn out, indifferent.

"The Party is growing."

"Obviously. But it doesn't matter."

"No. True. We have all the power on our side."

"So to speak, yes."

"Will there be clashes, do you think?"

"I'm sure there will be. At some point."

The conversation peters out. The weighty gentlemen get to their feet, shake hands and go their separate ways. Slow steps, eyes to the floor.

◆

"We were about fifteen kids and maybe ten adults at the gathering. Not exactly a mass meeting. The man from Blekinge who was speaking was going to go around various different properties. But then it ended up just being this one meeting. Turned out he had to leave. He stood on a barrel and we were a little way off and the little kids were running around, but he didn't mind that. We were impressed that he could speak for so long without any notes. He had a good voice. He didn't shout like some others. And I'd say we understood quite a lot. Everyone clapped. I and a few others bought his newspaper. He said the money would be spent on publishing more material. Then he went around asking what our jobs were, if we were in the Party, how much we earned. Many told him what a hellish life they had and he agreed. I imagine he was very intelligent and I suppose we felt just as we were meant to. Important and strong. I kept that paper for many years afterwards."

◆

"But there was a rift. I was told I could not stay at home if I became a socialist."

◆

Where was his mother? Was she sitting in the kitchen too and listening? Did she say anything? And his siblings?

◆

Oskar is brown from the sun. It has been a warm summer. The eyelids that have grown shut over the left eye socket shine a pale brown.

◆

Oskar Johannes Johansson. Oskar after the king. Johannes after his grandfather. Oskar never met him. He died in 1886, at the age of ninety-three.

◆

"If I'd been born a little earlier, I would have known someone who was born in the eighteenth century. He came from a small place up by Lake Boren. He worked on the construction of the Göta Canal. Once that was done, he got a job on one of the locks. He stayed and worked at that for the rest of his life. I believe they had six children, but only my father survived. I went there at some point in the thirties. The lock is still there and I expect it looks much the same as it always has. We cycled to it one summer, my boy and I. We spent an entire day watching all the traffic passing through the lock. We saw four timber boats, a ship from Lidköping carrying bricks and the passenger steamer coming by. If we'd had any money, we would probably have taken that boat back to Söderköping and then cycled home from there. But it was too expensive.

I didn't have any work at the time. It was interesting to look at it all, though.

"We also went to the churchyard and managed to find the gravestone. The inscription reads 'Johannes Johansson'. Underneath, it says 'Brita Johansson'. She seems to have died almost ten years before him. There were no pictures of them so I have no idea what they looked like. But then Far went to Norrköping. Like so many others, he wanted to move into town when the factories came. But Far became one of those who emptied out privies. He had no other work as long as he lived. There was nothing unusual about him, I suppose. He did what he had to. And didn't think it would be possible to get a better job. How he must have resented it. He slaved away his entire life without any respite. He would have had plenty of time to think. He died in 1936. He too grew to a ripe old age."

◆

Oskar Johannes Johansson has been a worker all his life. Like his father. Like his grandfather. Lock worker, canal construction worker. Privy worker. Rock blaster, rock blaster. Johannes, Oskar's father, Oskar.

Oskar's son has a laundry business in town. It belongs to him. The telephone directory lists him as a company director.

◆

It was a ramshackle wooden house, grey and draughty like the others that were crowded together side by side. At the back they all had the same kind of yard with a wooden shack that was part-privy, part-woodshed. The shacks were connected by a high plank fence which teetered on the very edge of a thirty-metre drop. Down below, the railway line ran into and out of town.

Axel Johansson lived with his family on the second floor of one of the wooden houses. A kitchen, one other room. The apartment had two windows and both gave out onto the yard. The parents had their bed in the room. The children slept in the kitchen. Oskar in a small wooden bed which was put out on the landing during the day. Karl in the kitchen sofa under the window, and Anna slept in the other wooden sofa on the far side of the dining table. There was so little room in the kitchen that it was barely possible for more than two people to move around in it at the same time. In the evenings, when everyone was at home, some of them sat in the kitchen and some on the bed in the room. That way you could sit and talk from one room to the other. It was a cold and draughty flat. However much you fired up the stove, it was never possible to raise the temperature to more than 12 degrees in winter.

◆

Oskar provides precious little information. The narrator has to piece together fragments to form a dull whole. Any snippets are delivered incidentally, when Oskar is talking about other things.

◆

"It was the same as all the other housing for workers. No better, no worse. Since we were an unusually small number of children, I imagine we were less cramped than many others. But in any case, we didn't know anything else. And there was nothing else to look forward to. You had the hovels which we workers crowded into and froze in. You had those big, light apartments in the stone buildings in the centre of town. You had the detached houses with their gardens. But to me those all seemed so remote that I hardly even thought about it until after the accident, which is when I first began to think at all.

"I remember that one night eleven more people slept in our apartment. There'd been a fire somewhere in town and everyone had to help out. I just don't know how it was possible to fit in another two adults and nine children. Even if it was only for one night. I suppose they must have lain there crying. After all, they had lost everything. And you could never easily find another place. The wooden houses were always overflowing. And there was nothing else. I have only a faint memory of it. I wasn't old when it happened."

◆

That is how Oskar lived.

That is how Elly lived.

Her sister.

The rock blasters.

All the others.

◆

But the workers' parties were growing. The right to vote, to housing, to decent working hours, pay. Society was awakening, its nerves beginning to twitch.

♦

But there is one detail in the narrative to do with the flat, with Oskar's childhood, which features more prominently than anything else.

It is a stone, which Johannes Johansson found during one of the years he was working on the construction of the canal. It is a piece of granite, perfectly round. But on one side there is a red crack which runs through the rock like a cross. The stone fits into a hand. And the cross is red against the greyish white of the stone. Axel Johansson took it with him when he moved to town. When he died, Oskar got it. Now it lies beside the transistor radio on the green wax tablecloth.

"Don't think that I want to have it on my grave. But I do think it is beautiful."

♦

I hold it in my hand and try to gauge its significance. It is a memento. Oskar's father carried it in his pocket or in a bundle when he walked the gravel roads into town. It has spent a lifetime on a chest of drawers indoors. Now it is in Oskar's cabin. A chip has broken off the back.

♦

"It's always been missing. When we were children, I suppose we must have asked how it had happened. But it always had a chip missing."

♦

The stone is like a crystal ball. Hold it in your hand, lower your gaze to look into the pale grey granite and the red cross.

◆

The summer after Oskar died, one June day, we roll the sauna away on logs. There are five of us. We heave the house onto a cattle barge and then tow it to the other side of the island, where it is to stand from now on. After one day of hard work it's in its place, under some tall oaks, right on top of a rocky knoll. The weather is hot and we don't finish until late in the evening.

At five in the morning I walk along the shore, skirt the steep cliffs and reach Oskar's headland. The mist is swirling and my boots sink deep into the soft soil.

◆

The four cornerstones. The ground between them is a mat of dead, yellow grass. There is a rusty oven door lying there, a black stove-pipe with large holes in it. Shards of glass, a couple of akvavit bottle tops. A rusty tin, used for worms. When I turn it upside down, spongy grey strips of moss fall out. A stiff worm lies at the bottom of the tin, which makes it look as if it is cracked. In the cellar, a pit dug into the earth, is an empty beer bottle.

◆

I walk up behind the cornerstones and take down the grey line with clothes pegs on it.

It is a fine summer. Soon the grass will be tall. And shrubs will be growing over the oven door and the stove-pipe.

I sit in the green flat-bottomed hardboard rowing boat. Row away from the headland.

In the late fifties a postcard photographer travelled through the archipelago. He went around the islands in October, and the cards are cold and off-putting. They are all black-and-white and sold poorly. A few years later colour postcards arrived and the black-and-white ones were piled up in the shops, unsold.

There is one postcard of the island. You can just see the sauna, appearing like a black piece of stage scenery among the bare branches of the trees. The photographer must have been about thirty metres from the shore when he took the picture.

As I look at the postcard, I imagine that I see the door ajar.

◆

"I remember the first time I met Norström. He wasn't quite as fat then as later on. They were busy blasting to clear the way for a main road. I got there in the middle of the day."

"If you want to be a rock blaster, you're going to have to put your back into it, matey."

"I think I can do that."

"Good. Norström's my name."

◆

Oskar Johannes Johansson. Helper, rock blaster, rock blaster again. Married to Elly's sister. One son, two daughters.

◆

Oskar buys lottery tickets. He has a standing order at the news-stand on the mainland. The mail boat brings him a ticket once a month. He wins nearly every time. Fifty or twenty-five kronor, never more. The following day his order goes in with the mail boat. It comes by at half past six. Oskar stands in the doorway and waves. That means he wants a bottle of akvavit.

In the evening, when the day's work is done, the mail boat ties up at the island. The mailman goes up to the cabin.

That evening we do not put out any nets.

"We were warned off alcohol at home. Far never drank. And the people who taught us to become socialists were also against drinking. I don't think I tasted any spirits until I turned forty."

They are sitting in the sauna, Oskar and the postman. Two glasses and some fizzy lemonade. The mailman, who lives on a nearby island, sweeps off his uniform cap. Sometimes, when Oskar has waved from the doorway in the morning, he spends the evening with Oskar in the sauna.

◆

What do they talk about?
     Mail. Letters. The strange things some people send.
     Fishing.
     They sit in silence.
     When the bottle is empty, the mailman makes for home.

♦

"It's a bloody nuisance that I have to do a morning round as well. Sometimes that's three hours' work for just one post-card."

"I see."

"The rubbish people write. I usually read the cards."

"Blimey!"

♦

Oskar's expressions. Again and again, with a touch of dialect.

Blimey.

I wonder.

I see.

God willing.

Blimey.

♦

"A number of times this summer I've come across boxes with hedgehogs in them. People don't seem to have the slight-est idea. Summer visitors don't understand that hedgehogs rarely survive the winter out here. When they come back the year after, they think the place will be swarming with hedge-hogs. But of course it isn't."

Then they talk about all the hornets this summer. The ones in the old boathouse. The size of your thumb. Vicious now in the autumn.

At their most poisonous in spring?

Like everything else, it no doubt varies.

The mailman is talking. Oskar answers.

"Blimey."

"I see."

◆

Pike pest.

"It's spread to cod now as well. You can't even throw them back. They have to be buried. That means bloody standing and digging holes for the fish every day. Must be all the crap in the water. One morning I nearly ran into a chest of drawers floating there. It's crazy."

◆

Akvavit makes Oskar tired. After he's had a few, he sleeps for a long time. The mailman helps him to bed. Then he goes down to his boat, which has been lying there with the motor running all that time, the regular thump of the fuel-oil engine.

When Oskar wakes up in the morning, he goes out and lies down on the ground under an oak tree. His snoring can be heard across the bay. The red wood-ants crawl all over him. Sometimes he sleeps until midday.

◆

Oskar suddenly stops his rowing and breathing. Then he points with the left oar and says:

"What's that?"

I turn and look. The flounders are flapping weakly on the floor of the boat.

I see something white floating in the water, ten metres away.

"Shall we take a look?"

Oskar rows over and I lean out from the boat and take hold of the white object.

◆

As we row home, we have a few sodden logbooks lying in the boat. Later, when we take a closer look, we see that they come from a German vessel. M.S. *Matilda*, Bremen.

"The captain was probably drunk and fed up."

I sit there and try to decipher the washed-out sentences and numbers in the books. The pages stick together and it is hard to separate them. Figures, positions, cargoes, ports. I read them aloud for Oskar. We have the door open and mosquitoes are dancing in the room. Oskar raises his head and looks at them.

"They don't bother me. Let them have a little blood."

◆

On a calm night every two weeks or so we burn rubbish. So the logbooks go up in flames along with the plastic bags, leftover food, and newspapers. The plastic spreads its acrid smell and Oskar hits out at the smoke with his walking stick.

"I had to start using it ten years ago. The injuries to my stomach began to hurt again and the best way of easing the pain was to lean forward when I walked. The stick helped."

It is light brown with a rubber ferrule on the end.

"This is my summer cane. I have another one at home in town. It's black."

◆

Now Oskar is dead. At the time I saw the cane as a yellow stick, with a black rubber cover over the end and a worn handle.

Now I remember the words "summer cane".

Summer cane. Lying across the blue-covered knees.

Summer cane.

Winter cane?

◆

Oskar does not want a metal hook in place of his blown-off hand. Neither does he want to have an enamel eye inserted into the empty eye socket. He wants to have a stump for an arm and his eyelids to be sewn together.

◆

He is skinny and pale when he leaves hospital. He walks gingerly. He looks at the ground in front of him, tests each step, sets one foot in front of the other and does not notice the looks from the passers-by. The reactions at the sight of his eye socket. The grimaces at the stump of his arm sticking out of his coat sleeve.

Oskar is discharged from hospital in January. It is very cold and the hard snow crunches under his feet. Breath steams from his mouth and his earlobes are burning. Oskar leaves hospital on foot.

♦

The game of Patience does not work out. Oskar rakes the cards together to begin again.

♦

What about the time in between?

There were years, events. From 1910 to 1965, to 1969. There is an ever-shifting reality, an ever-changing Oskar. He has been a disabled worker all along. Has had the same life as everyone else. Brutal swings between having work and being laid off. He has more money. Better accommodation. Society changes and Oskar changes. Oskar never talks about development. He talks about change and the narrator thinks that it is exactly the right word for what he means. Oskar is a worker. He belongs to a group that he sees as clearly defined and also clearly segregated. There are those key words again. They keep surfacing. Key words, cropping up time and again, marking the stages in Oskar's life by something other than years. And it is some of the changes, never the violent ones but those that take their time, which divide up Oskar's life. Once again. Certain key words. The games that were the same. I've been a worker all my life. Everything has changed, but not for us. Oskar simply sees himself for what he is. He keeps emphasising that there was never anything out of the ordinary about him, but he never says what he means by out of the ordinary. He says he is one of the others. Nothing more. A rock blaster with a family. Who matters to his family but not to anybody or anything else. He does not feel that he has had anything to do with any of the changes. They happened and they have had an effect. But he himself had no part in shaping them. The worker is a member of his community, but the forces driving and changing society are wielded by others. That is what Oskar really means when he says that there is nothing out of the ordinary about him.

◆

That is where we disagree.

Magnus Nilsson

Magnus Nilsson was the name of Oskar's workmate and Oskar moved in with him the year before the accident. Nilsson had an identical apartment to the one in which Oskar had lived. The wooden houses were built on the same plan. Where there was room, they had sprung up, keeping pace with the growth of industry. At first they were on the outskirts, but they then gradually became part of the centre as the towns grew around them. Magnus Nilsson lived in another neighbourhood, and it was there that Oskar moved when he was no longer allowed to stay at home because he had become a socialist. Magnus worked on the same team of blasters as Oskar and he was one of the men who stood looking at the hand among the dandelions. Magnus had always lived in the same apartment. After the death of their parents the children had stayed on there until, one after the other, they moved away and Magnus alone was left. He had never married. He was now forty-five years old and beginning to show signs of exhaustion. He was taciturn, short and quite stocky. He had a coarse, angular face. His brown eyes were set deep under drooping eyelids and his hair was black and tangled. He was a skilled hand and easy to work with.

It was Magnus who, during a lunch break, asked Oskar whether he wanted to move into his home and share the apartment. The blasters were lying drowsing under the birch trees some distance away from where they were working. They were blasting in preparation for a bridge which was to be built over the railway line.

◆

Without knowing it they found themselves at the back of the very hillock that was to have a tunnel dug through it the following year. A muted, laconic exchange. They are lying on their backs in the grass with their eyes half shut. One of them asks if anyone has been to listen to the agitator.

"Yes. He was good."

Oskar props himself up on his elbows.

"He said how important it was for us to join the Party. When I got home, Farsan told me I'd have to move out if I became a socialist."

Magnus lying with eyes shut. Without moving, he says:

"Are you a socialist?"

"Yes."

"You can move into my place. There's room. You can have the kitchen to yourself."

The conversation becomes a dialogue between Magnus Nilsson and Oskar Johansson. The others doze off as soon as the conversation no longer concerns them. One of them falls asleep and snores softly.

"Do you mean it?"

"Yes. You can move in whenever you want."

After work, Magnus and Oskar go off together. There are twenty-two years and thirty centimetres between them.

◆

A fortnight later, Oskar moves in. With two bundles. One in each hand. He arrives at nine in the evening. Magnus makes them coffee and Oskar makes a bed for himself in the kitchen sofa.

"Locking up won't be a problem since we come and go at the same time."

"Decent of you."

"There's plenty of space."

◆

When Oskar left home with his bundles there was silence. His father was not back yet and his mother does not feature in Oskar's accounts. His sister and brother were there. His sister and brother were not there. His mother was there. His mother was not there.

◆

Then they sit at the kitchen table and carefully sound each other out. They are going to live together. By asking some practical questions they get a feel for one another.

"We'll have to share everything. It'll all fall into place as we go along."

"Can you cook?"

"Well I've lived on my own for a long time. I'm happy to go on doing the meals. Nothing to it. Just ordinary food."

"Do you need to be woken up?"

"Not at all."

Oskar asks about Elly.

"Naturally. That's fine."

"It'll only be every now and then. The odd Thursday."

"That'll be fine. It won't bother me."

Oskar asks about other things and Magnus answers. Soon they know each other. Soon they can start to talk.

◆

Oskar talks about Magnus with great affection. There are two words he often uses, alone and exhausted.

"Of course it was very exciting to be living on my own. That's how it felt even though there were two of us. Magnus was not the sort of person one ever noticed. When we got home from work, we were tired and once we'd eaten and washed the dishes, we went to bed. On Sundays I was out and about. Magnus was always home when I got back. I don't think he'd set foot outside all day. He sat in his room doing jigsaw puzzles. Or else reading some newspaper."

◆

As we know, Magnus was a socialist. Sometimes he would comment on something he had heard or read and then he always ended by saying that socialism would change all that.

"Do you really think so? How?"

"Through revolution. It's bound to happen. It goes without saying."

"When?"

"Soon. In ten years."

"How can you be so sure?"

"It goes without saying."

"I find it hard to believe."

"It isn't hard. We've been organising ourselves for twenty years now. And all along people have come to a better understanding of what socialism will do for them. As individuals, that is. The bourgeoisie call it murder, but that's not what it's about. It's about getting us more food and better housing and things like that. We need to have a share in the means of production. We can't let things go on as they are. It goes without saying."

•

It goes without saying.

How did Oskar answer? Did it go without saying, or did he really understand?

"But how's it going to happen? Are we going to fight?"

"We have to! They're not going to give anything away. If they do, there's a catch somewhere. Then they've tricked us."

"Fight? How?"

"With weapons."

"What weapons?"

"It goes without saying. We've got to get those who have weapons on our side."

"The police?"

"Them too. Some of them. Enough of them."

"Do you really think so?"

"Their lives will improve too."

"And the military?"

"Well, the soldiers are workers on military service, after all."

"But what about the captains? The others. The lieutenants?"

"How many of them are there?"

"No, that's clear, I understand that . . . But when do we start?"

"When we're strong enough."

"How will we know?"

"We'll know. It'll be obvious."

◆

Oskar is lying on his sofa.

Oskar is lying in his old officer's bed.

He is awake.

◆

"I always liked Magnus. You could rely on him. He was a fine worker. A good mate."

The trade union's register of members still exists. They're listed there. Johansson, Johansson, Karlsson, Lundgren, Larsson, Larsson, Marklund, Moqvist, Nilsson, Nilsson, Nilsson, Nilsson.

There are two M. Nilssons. One of them is Magnus Nilsson.

Elvira, Elly's Sister

Magnus Nilsson meets Elly several times. But he is also there when Oskar marries her sister. Oskar is happy and puts his mutilated arm around Magnus' shoulders.

◆

Elly, sister.

Elvira, sister.

◆

"We met at a protest march. There were actually many who did in those days. And perhaps that wasn't surprising. It was one of the few occasions we were all together at the same time. And you never knew who you would end up walking next to. You laughed at each other and said something. Then when the meeting was over, we had to get back to town. Nothing odd about that. It may sound a bit strange, but it wasn't.

"We chatted and she clearly wasn't bothered by the way I looked. In those days there were many who were injured. Sooner or later it happened to almost all workers. Many had had rickets. Others had coughing fits as we marched and sang and some even had to sit down by the side of the procession to get their strength back. Some were limping. Quite a few had lost a whole arm. I remember that for years there was an old man who carried one of the banners with his one arm. He was incredibly strong. The other arm had been torn off by a cutting machine. Right up by his shoulder. And there were many women too who were missing an arm or some fingers. It was almost normal. We used to go for coffee after marching. I suppose I must have asked if she would let me invite her. She replied that her name was Elvira and said, yes please. We went to some café. She told me she worked in the textile factory. She used to spin raw wool. She lived at home with her parents. They were seven children. She may have mentioned that one of them was called Elly, but I didn't think anything of it. We talked about the demonstration. I remember her saying that she only knew the first verse of the song we'd been singing. She found reading so difficult, she said. And then I suddenly noticed that she kept narrowing her eyes because she couldn't see properly. I asked her why she didn't wear glasses and she said that then she would lose her job. But what about after work, I asked. She was afraid that some foreman would see her with them on. She did have a pair at home, however. It seems that her poor eyesight was congenital.

"Afterwards I walked her home. We decided to meet again the week after. She lived quite far out of town, where the houses were among the oldest and most dilapidated. I was actually quite pleased to have met her.

"I had no idea she was Elly's sister. It was a strange coincidence."

·

When Elvira died, Elly came to the funeral. She and Oskar sat next to each other at the crematorium. Oskar's children sat behind. Then when Elly died, just one year later, Oskar saw it in the newspaper. Otherwise, he would have attended. I know that without him telling me.

·

There are sticky rings from beer bottles on the table. The place is quite full and Oskar sits in a corner nodding at the people who come and go. Most of them are men. It is an evening in the middle of the week.

Then Elvira arrives and many eyes turn to her as she stands in the doorway and looks for Oskar. When Elvira goes over and sits down at his table, there are some who smile and wink and nod at Oskar.

They order coffee. They stir their cups and this time it is harder for them to talk to each other.

·

Elvira is wearing a white dress. Elly gave it to her.

"That's a nice dress."

"You think so?"

"White looks nice. Would you like some more?"

"Yes, thanks. Thank you, that's enough."

"Don't you take sugar?"

"No. Never."

"I do. Always."

"It tastes better without."

"You think?"

They are sitting in the café and there is a buzz and a clatter. A grating sound of chairs scraping over the wooden floor. Cups and glasses chink.

Then comes the question and Oskar is expecting it.

◆

"A blasting accident a year ago. The newspapers actually wrote that I was dead. But I made it."

"How did it feel?"

"I don't remember. Everybody asks me, but I have no memory of it. It all just went white I think. Like your dress."

Elvira giggles and looks down. Oskar asks her how old she is.

"Twenty-two this year."

"I'm twenty-four."

"I thought you were older."

"I'm not."

Spoons stirring.

"Can I see you on Sunday?"

"I've got to look after my brothers and sisters so that Mor and Far can go to church."

"Why don't I help you?"

"Do you want to?"

"Yes. If you like."

"Well, come at eleven then."

◆

After that they walk around town for a while. The seventh of May, 1912.

◆

Elvira pours out coffee. Oskar is wearing his best clothes and sitting at the kitchen table. The younger brothers and sisters romp around. Elvira wants to show that she is firm and tells them not to jump about so much and to make less noise. Oskar says it doesn't bother him.

They exchange a few sentences to get to the most important thing.

"When can we see each other again?"

"Some evening."

"Wednesday?"

"Thursday's better."

And Oskar begins to take Elvira out on Thursday evenings.

◆

He tells Magnus about Elvira. Magnus gives a little smile and nods.

"We might come back here for a while."

"Do. I can go out."

"No. You don't need to."

"I'm quite happy to. As long as it doesn't get too late."

"It won't."

◆

And Elvira does come. They sit there even more quietly. They sit at the kitchen table, and only just before Elvira has to leave

Oskar reaches out and takes her hand. Left hand, left hand. Elvira is prepared for it.

◆

By writing in to a magazine advice column or calling the Swedish Meteorological Institute, you can find out what the weather was like then. Was it raining as Elvira walked home? The newspaper archives reveal that the textile industry in which Elvira worked was doing well, with strong sales and high production figures.

◆

But they are sitting at the kitchen table. Left hand in left hand. Empty coffee cups. A fly buzzing in the window. Magnus Nilsson walking along the streets.

◆

It hurts when Oskar has to pee. He feels a tightening and tugging in his abdomen. It is a pain that he will have to live with. But now he is lying on the kitchen sofa. Magnus is snoring in his room. Elvira left several hours ago. Soon they will all be working at their different places. Oskar feels his penis starting to rise. It has begun to heal and the doctors have said that he can have children. It rises and Oskar senses that it is short. But it does lift and stiffen. Oskar reaches for it with his hand. He thinks about Elvira and then realises that he can function.

◆

He gets up for a while. Sits down at the kitchen table in his nightshirt, and dreams.

◆

"I began picking her up from work whenever I could make it. The smell there was awful. Just next door there was some factory where they made something which stank. Elvira worked in a sooty brick building. I remember that I used to press my ear against the wall and then you could hear the machines inside. You felt the walls vibrating. Then, as soon as the siren started to howl, they all came pouring out at the same time. It looked as if they were running away. Elvira was never among the first. She used to wash very carefully. Many of them never bothered. They must have been too tired. Or else they wanted to get away as quickly as possible. When the siren began to blare, I used to cross over to the other side of the street and wait there. I suppose that was a bit childish. I was always nervous before she came out through the factory gate. It was one of the times when I met her there that she told me Elly was her sister."

◆

When Oskar returned to the blasting team he was received with great respect.

"You're welcome back. We want you to know that."

Norström is standing there, tall and heavy, and slaps Oskar on the shoulder.

"From now on it's you who blows up the dynamite, and not the other way round."

Norström's laughs his loud rumbling laugh.

"And we don't have to do those bloody tunnels anymore. No need to make holes which end up collapsing sooner or later. Every single piece of rock has to go."

Norström points. They are blasting along the main road. It is to be widened.

"I don't see the point. It's not as though we're so crowded that we can't all fit on the road. But never mind. As long as we get to blast it all away."

Then the work begins again. Oskar does what he can, given his handicap. He bakes dynamite, he primes charges, he takes care of detonating cables and explosions. But when a charge does not go off, it is one of the others who goes to check. Others carry the metal spikes. Others take the cart and the shovels. Norström walks around, kicks at the young helper, who is new.

"You see that, Johansson. The last one got so scared when you were blown in the air that he quit. Weaklings."

Norström yells at everybody except Oskar. Oskar's accident is the gem in Norström's life as a rock blaster. Oskar is a blaster again. For the second time in his life.

◆

One evening Norström asks Oskar to his home. He has invited colleagues, blasting bosses from other teams, and Oskar will be on show. Amid boozing and bragging.

Oskar arrives at about seven. The same wooden house, the same flat, but always somewhere else in town. The children have been turned out. The wife stays in the back room.

The foremen are in the kitchen, sitting around the table.

"Here's Johansson. You're to shake him by the hand, and show him some bloody respect."

Norström's face is puce. He is sweating from the alcohol coursing through his veins. Three other foremen sit around the table. All the same age as Norström. Somehow, they all look alike. The same sagging bellies. The same huge fists. The same booming voices.

◆

"Sit down here next to me."

Norström kicks out a chair. Oskar sits. The men peer at him.

"So you're the one who survived that bang. Well done."

"Well done? That's putting it mildly."

Norström shows off his gem. Glasses are filled and drained.

"Aren't you having anything?"

"No, thanks."

"Don't be stupid. Whoever heard of a blaster turning down a snaps?"

Norström booms.

"Well, I suppose you have an excuse, after your accident. Have a beer." Oskar sits with his glass while the foremen gradually turn to vying with each other over performance, curious episodes involving dynamite, eccentric blasters, terrible accidents. Oskar listens.

"We had one who blew himself up. I guess he'd got himself plastered. During the lunch break he took some dynamite, lit it and stuck it in his pocket. There was nothing left of him. I think we found half a shoe."

"Bloody hell."

"Bloody hell."

"Some time in 1890 we lost two blasters in one day. One accident in the morning and another in the afternoon. And they were brothers. For a while I think we suspected that the one in the afternoon had done it on purpose. Presumably he was upset about what had happened to his brother."

Then the conversation moves on to socialism.

"We should take care of the Party."

"But why the hell paint everything so black? To call the king a traitor and murderer is going a bit far, isn't it? They went to jail, didn't they?"

"Yes. We collected money for them."

"There's bound to be a revolution. Don't you agree, Johansson?"

"It goes without saying."

"It does indeed."

◆

Oskar believes in the revolution. That is Magnus Nilsson's doing. He has found a new way to talk to him about it. He has made Oskar restive. Change is possible. There has to be change. The way things are now is just wrong and unfair. And restive people soon begin to make demands.

When Oskar leaves the foremen he goes home, but at the same time he is walking towards a different experience of reality.

The Party Member

This story skims the surface. It is recounted in few words, as spare in its telling as Oskar himself is. It has cracks and gaps. But the surface has pores in it. Gradually it begins to turn and open up. And under the surface lies this story.

The story of the changes.

◆

Hjalmar Branting. Party leader.

Oskar Johansson. Party member.

Per Albin Hansson. Party leader.

Oskar Johansson. Party member.

Tage Erlander. Party leader.

Oskar Johansson. Rock blaster who has left the Party.

Olof Palme. Party leader.

Hilding Hagberg. Party leader.

Oskar Johansson. Party member, former rock blaster.

C. H. Hermansson. Party leader.

Oskar Johansson. Party member, former rock blaster. Widower, pensioner.

◆

Oskar is even-tempered. I know him as someone who never

gets angry, who laughs a lot, who is an optimist. I know him to be stable.

Was it always so? Once he tells me the old joke about the man who says: I've never been a pessimist. I've been an optician all my life. He tells it as if the story were about him.

It may be. But the narrator has his doubts.

◆

Was it always so?

No. It was not.

◆

"Elvira and I never argued. I don't think we said a harsh word to each other during all the years we had together. I suppose we scolded the children when they were little and making a racket, but we never hit them. Elvira and I always agreed. We never needed to discuss anything. We wanted the same things. But there's nothing out of the ordinary about that."

The Iceberg

In the summer of 1912, the Olympic Games are held in Stockholm. The blasters are sitting under the birch trees, discussing the results.

As yet not one of them can imagine that they would ever be able to attend the Games.

•

This story becomes anecdotal. The fragments are fragments. Oskar lives, is dead, is to be buried, has been buried, lives again. But his reality is always a continuum. There are no gaps there, no cracks, no spaces in the margins. Oskar Johansson's reality is a matter of the struggle between capitalism and socialism, between revolution and reformism. That has been the stuff of Oskar Johansson's life. Oskar Johansson regards himself as insignificant, significant, insignificant again.

•

What were the causes?

What was the political evolution that is Oskar's life?

•

1968. Oskar talks about what is happening in Paris, in Berlin. He talks about America. He is sitting in the cabin, a few days before I am due to leave and we are never to meet again. He is sitting in the sauna, it is autumn and the paraffin lamp gives off a warm light. He has just changed the wick and topped up with paraffin. Our faces and movements cast shadows against the wall. We can hear the wind outside, it is pitch black and the waves are rolling against the shore. We hear a faint rumble from the sea crashing against the cliffs on the other side of the headland. The radio is on and we are listening to *Dagens Eko*. They have stepped up the bombing raids again. The voice on the radio sounds harsh and dry in the room. Oskar is listening. His arms resting on the table.

◆

His head is bent forward. He has his summer cane across his knees, over his blue work trousers. When the *Eko* ends, the finger presses the button. There is silence. The ocean beats against the island. Then Oskar gives his brief comments about the bombs. He never raises his head. His index finger is still.

"They're crazy. You'd think the devil really exists, at least when you hear what they're doing down there. What do they think they can achieve? They can kill a load of people. But there are quite a few of us."

◆

I get up and we shake hands as we do when I arrive and when I leave. We nod, say that we'll see each other next year, and

I walk into the night. The wind is lashing and tearing. It is dark and hard to see. There is salt in the air.

◆

The story of Oskar is like an iceberg. What you see is only a small part. Most of it is hidden under the surface. That is where the bulk of the ice is, keeping its balance in the water and making its speed and course steady.

The story consists of two strands which run in parallel. A few summers' worth of events and memories shared with a retired rock blaster. Then we have the course of history, the developments that changed the society in which Oskar lived. He talks about his affinity with the first strand, and ignores the other. It is a fault line where two plates grind against each other, two cogwheels mesh with each other. The two of them reflect the same evolution. They are mirror images of each other. They share a single identity. They describe the features of the society that is Oskar Johansson's.

◆

Oskar Johansson's face.

The narrator's face.

Together they become the story.

◆

There is salt in the air. The wind tears at my eyes and I walk through the forest instead of following the shoreline. It is like walking through a black wall. Bushes and branches beat against my face. The juniper pricks, the birches whip.

◆

It is the early autumn of 1968. The narrator has visited Oskar Johansson for the last time.

The Pensioner

Once he tells me about his last day at work. He left his job at six o'clock on September 14, 1954. He stood in the yellow changing hut with a bunch of flowers in his hand. It consisted of two tulips and three green twigs. He held the flowers pinched between thumb and index finger and heard one of the assistant directors of the construction company speak. The air was muggy and hot because of the bad ventilation and the stench from the damp raincoats and boots. There were nine of them in the cramped little hut. From his description, I get the impression that it was even smaller than the cabin which to all intents and purposes later became Oskar's home.

Oskar had intended to go on working until Christmas that year, but then he changed his mind.

◆

"I just don't know why. But the closer it got, the more pointless it seemed to keep on working, since I didn't have to. So one Friday I told them. Next week will be my last. They didn't really say anything. Even in those days there was no room at work for older men. So don't think there's anything new about this idea that you're old before you're even forty. But there weren't so many people then."

◆

When the cleaner came to clear up the hut at four in the morning on September 15, the flowers were still on the table. Oskar never says whether he left them there on purpose or forgot them.

◆

"The flowers never made it home. I suppose they got left behind."

◆

On September 15, Oskar stayed in bed. He lay there and listened to the trams clanking past in the street and was glad not to have to go outside in the slush. He clearly remembers how it rained that morning. He remembers that it was a sustained, heavy downpour, and he remembers the awning on the balcony of the apartment above flapping in the wind.

He lay in his bed and heard the mail thump down into the letterbox. He felt no regret that his work was over. He lay there thinking that next year, next summer, he would move out early to the archipelago.

◆

In the afternoon he leaves the apartment and buys a calendar. He has never done that before. But now he buys one which he hangs up in the kitchen. It is a tear-off calendar where one page has to be removed every day. With a large disc that he rotates once every month. The theme on the disc changes according to the seasons. For September that year, 1954, there is a black-and-white picture of people in rain gear waiting for a yellow number 34 bus.

◆

When the assistant director has finished his speech, he pats Oskar on the shoulder and calls for three cheers. A roar goes up in the hut and then the assistant director leaves. After that, Oskar and his workmates start to change to go home. Oskar throws his blue work trousers into a box which serves as a rubbish bin. They lie there among sausage skins and greaseproof paper.

Then they all go off, one after the other.

"Have a nice time, then. In this weather."

"Thanks."

"Only two more years to go."

"They'll pass quickly."

"Let's hope so."

"Thanks for all our time together."

"You too."

Then they all leave the hut and pick their way across the muddy ground. Some take their bicycles, others practically run away. Oskar walks towards the tram stop.

◆

"Can't for the life of me remember what he said. It wasn't much. But there was something about the accident."

◆

Oskar and the accident always go together. Everyone mentions it as Oskar's distinguishing feature.

"An old boy who was blown up but somehow managed to survive."

"A thumb that looks bloody awful. But he's a decent sort."

"He certainly gets by in spite of it."

◆

Oskar hardly ever talks about the accident. On the rare occasions that he does, he sounds hesitant and not at all forthcoming and gives the impression of being disconnected from what once happened.

◆

Oskar is lying in bed. It is the evening of September 15, 1954. He has switched off the bedside light and lies there in the half-dark, looking out into the room. Then he gets to his feet and goes into the kitchen. He takes a pencil from the kitchen table and draws a little cross over September 13. He puts down the pencil and goes back to bed.

The following day, when he is having his coffee, he notices that he marked the wrong date, but he does not bother to change it.

◆

"All of that autumn and winter, I sat and waited for spring. I don't think I did anything else. But I had a yearning in me and you can live on that for a long time. Not only when you are young.

"The days passed. I mostly just waited. And luckily the winter was short that year. So it wasn't too long."

◆

When Oskar leaves the Social Democratic Party, it is no sudden and dramatic decision, rather the result of a long series of developments. But when he talks about it, it is mainly because of his feeling that too little happened over too long a period of time. He never explains exactly what he means. All he says is that something came to a standstill. And since Oskar only very rarely discusses the reasons for the changes he himself has brought about, all he really mentions are the words "standstill" and "too slow". He makes no comparisons between the party he leaves and the one he joins. All he does is change his party membership.

◆

But once, one evening in August during one of the last summers, he says that his pension has increased and adds in passing that he has often found that one never has anything to lose by changing one's opinions, if necessary. He says that one can easily change party once a year if one really thinks it worthwhile.

"But your pension? How do you mean?"

"It's gone up."

"Yes?"

"Well, it should have gone up even more. You know what food costs."

"Yes, of course. I know."

"Well. Precisely."

◆

For a couple of summers, Oskar regularly listens to radio drama. One evening, he tunes in for the first time, and after that he repeats the experience a couple of times a week. This continues over two summers. But the third summer, he no longer listens. Not that he switches over to some other programme. The radio stands there silent. Instead, he has started to solve crossword puzzles. He has picked out a dozen or so of them from old newspapers under his bed. He has torn them out and put them on the table in front of the radio. He starts in May and by one of the last days in August he has solved them all, and as we burn rubbish one evening, I see them catch fire among the leftover food and cardboard.

◆

But one of the puzzles is left behind, has slipped down and got stuck behind the table. When the time comes to move the sauna after Oskar's death and the table is carried out, the yellowing piece of paper drops onto the floor.

He has solved the crossword. But I see that he has made a spelling mistake in one place and as a result has got the wrong words to fit in. He has written "ögonblick" without a "c". And after that, a whole section of the crossword is skewed, but he has still managed to fit in words so that the letters match even though the clues in fact referred to quite different words. He has solved his crossword puzzle and with his spelling mistake created a new one.

♦

The picture of Oskar is obscure. Contradictions and empty answers, silence and ambiguous pronouncements are just a part of the unfinished picture. Sometimes too, minor events break into the picture, opening up cracks, ensuring that all the way through the picture remains incomplete.

Sometimes I think Oskar is doing it deliberately.

At other times, I'm sure I'm wrong.

♦

Once I forget my wallet on the table. When I fetch it the next day and later want to take out a postage stamp, I find that it is gone.

Another time, as we are sitting in the gloom of the cabin with the radio turned off and his index finger drumming on the wax tablecloth, Oskar suddenly bangs his fist on the table and in a loud and tuneless voice starts to sing a few verses from the chapbook song "Elfsborg Fortress". He sits with his head bowed over the table and sings at the top of his voice. Then all of a sudden he stops, mid-verse, and the index finger begins to drum on the table again.

A third time Oskar asks me to buy him a pornographic magazine when I go to the mainland to do the shopping. First, he lists the usual things he wants. Milk, coffee, bread. But then he adds that he wants me to buy him a girlie magazine. He does not know of any particular title, and asks me to choose. When I return, I have bought *Kriminaljournalen* and *Cocktail*. His only comment is that one would have been enough.

Then he sits down and flicks through the magazines. He is not interested in the text. He just turns the pages, pausing for a brief moment at each picture. Then he continues, and when he has finished he simply puts them away with the other newspapers he has in the house.

A fourth time he is asleep when I arrive to take up the nets with him. He is breathing evenly and when he opens his eye and sees me in the doorway he just turns over and goes back to sleep.

◆

"I sometimes think it would be nice if it was all over."

◆

Only once do his words suggest that he is fed up and tired. It happens one beautiful day as we are sitting outside the cabin and the flies buzz around us. We are watching a fishing boat, packed with tourists, sail past and they wave at us. This time Oskar does not wave back with his stump of an arm. Instead, he raises his voice to be heard over the sound of the thumping engine.

◆

"I sometimes think it would be nice if it was all over."

◆

He says nothing more. Soon afterwards another boat comes past, equally full. This time he waves back.

◆

"I think I'll keep on waving."

"Yes."

"Because they look like a happy lot."

"They're on holiday now."

"That will soon be over."

"They're lucky with the weather."

"You can never be sure."

"But you can always hope."

"Yes."

◆

The picture of Oskar that never becomes complete is inextricably linked to the society in which he has lived. Oskar as a presence, but almost never a participant, runs like a red thread through the description he gives of himself. The incomplete fragments, the half-words, half-sentences, the short and disconnected episodes which he produces from his memory are his way of confirming what he means. The image he gives of himself is that of one who was present. But the person he is every day, during the years when we meet, is a participant. Oskar tries to create a false picture of himself, and his story has to be seen and developed in the context of whatever motivated this choice. One of our last summers together, I try to be more methodical in the way I put my questions, but it leads to the only episode of mistrust that ever arises between us. For a little more than a month he is reticent, taciturn even, sometimes a little gruff. But then one day he is back to normal again, stuttering out his own account of himself at irregular intervals. His words almost never seem to follow any thoughts he bears within himself, instead they give the impression of taking him by surprise, emerging from a room he would rather see closed and locked, slipping out almost unintentionally. Every memory, every word that has to do with his life is followed by a silence, which is scarcely noticeable. Then he sometimes goes on to talk about things we are busy with, but there is still a small silence behind the words. And in his telling, there is rarely any enthusiasm. What he says can sometimes be incredibly insistent, but he almost never raises or lowers his voice. Here the unexpected song, the sudden outburst with "Elfsborg Fortress", is a mysterious exception.

◆

Once Oskar said that he had not been to the cinema since the mid-thirties. I remember him saying that it had simply not appealed to him. Then I asked him something and he once more replied that he simply did not like it, and that he himself found that a bit odd.

◆

One summer, Oskar develops a strange itch where his eyelids have grown together. It gets so bad that he begins to scratch the scar at night and one morning he sees pus on his pillow. He travels to the hospital and is admitted for a week. The scar is opened up and the infection healed. Then the socket is sewn together again and he can return to the island. A week later he goes back for the day and has the stitches removed.

When he returns, he says the doctors told him that they found a tiny piece of grit embedded in the socket and that it had presumably been there ever since the accident. Oskar gives a knowing smile and unfolds a handkerchief. I see a greyish-white piece of grit on the white fabric. Then he blows it onto the floor and it vanishes.

"I took it with me so you could see." Then, just when I'm about to leave:

"In the olden days someone might have written a song about this grit in my eye."

◆

And the speck, which had been wrapped in the handkerchief, and bounced across the floor and disappeared down some crack, is the last episode I can remember. After that, there are no more memories clear enough for me to describe.

◆

The stone.
The piece of grit.
Those terse words.
All those summers.

Oskar Johansson,
Forty-Four Years Old

He went down the stone steps to the quayside. The air was raw and cold, a few days into September 1932. He walked carefully, keeping very close to the rusty handrail so as not to fall. He could feel how his right foot was damper than the left and saw a yawning hole in the seam between the sole and the rest of the shoe.

He cut across the quay and turned into the old residential area which climbed up the cliffs on one side of the harbour. He was walking quite briskly and knew that he did not need to be too careful. All the trolleys were lined up in rows outside the long grey lime-washed warehouses. The railway tracks were deserted and empty freight cars stood crowded on the sidings between the storehouses.

No ships were tied up along the dock. The quayside had large gaping cracks filled with the turbid black harbour water, viscous and polluted. He drew the sweetish smell of saltwater in through his nose and looked out over the port. All he could see there were the half-rotten barges for use when the harbour entrance was dredged every few years. A fishing vessel, some rowing boats. Nothing more.

When he reached the housing area, he turned onto a

narrow winding gravel path running between the ramshackle houses. He walked past the first of the two-storey houses and then stopped outside the third. He went in through the front door and walked over to the first entrance to the left on the ground floor.

He stood there in the faint light and knocked. The door was opened almost immediately.

◆

As soon as he came in, he saw Lindgren sitting in a corner of the kitchen sofa. There he was, pale and skinny, and it was obvious that he had not shaved for some weeks. As Oskar stood in the doorway, Lindgren gave him a lifeless look.

"Afternoon."

"Afternoon."

It was Lindgren's mother who let Oskar in. She was more than seventy and had shrunk so much that she hardly reached up to Oskar's chest. She held out her right hand, her brown arm like a weathered stick, and squeezed Oskar's thumb.

"Well, if it isn't Johansson come to visit. That's unexpected."

"I have the time now. I thought I'd say hello to Lindgren."

"How kind. He doesn't really see people now."

Lindgren sat there, staring dully and open-mouthed at Oskar and his mother. He was wearing a shirt with large checks and had broad braces which hung down his trouser legs. His hair was black and tangled and his large fists rested on the table.

Oskar looked at Lindgren. They had not seen each other

for nearly a year. Oskar could tell that Lindgren had got worse. His eyes were watery now and lacking any expression. The last time Oskar had met him, there had still been occasional signs of alertness about him, faint but unmistakable indications that the brain was still receiving impressions and process-ing them.

◆

Lindgren was suffering from an illness which was slowly but inexorably killing his brain. He had worked on the same blasting team with Oskar for many years, until his condition had made it impossible to have him along. Since then he had lived at home with his mother, sitting on the kitchen sofa and being fussed over by her. Her senses too had been deadened by everything she had inhaled over thirty-five years of labour in a dye-works, in addition to the arteriosclerosis that had crept up on her during the last year.

"Won't you sit down, Johansson?"

Oskar lowers himself onto the sofa next to Lindgren, who slowly turns his head and stares at him with empty eyes. His mother is standing in the middle of the small, run-down kitchen and looks at her son.

"Aren't you going to say hello to Johansson?"

She walks over to her son, somewhat irritated, and gives his shoulder a shove. He reacts slowly, stares at her.

"Don't you see that Johansson's come to visit you?"

Lindgren twists his head again and looks at Oskar.

"It's nice to see you here, Joha, but I must slee now can we ge cakesfee . . ."

His brain is unable to finish the sentence he has begun. He falls silent and stares down at the table.

Oskar gets to his feet. He has not taken off his outdoor clothes.

"I thought I'd take him out with me to get him some fresh air."

"Air?"

"I imagine he spends most of his days indoors. And I have time now."

"You're so kind, Johansson. Of course, the boy needs to get out. But in that case, I'll pack a basket with coffee and buns for you to take with you."

"Isn't it a bit cold now to be taking coffee outside? September's rather late for that."

◆

But Lindgren's mother already pictures her son on an outing with Oskar. She wastes no time in preparing coffee and some dry buns and tying it all up in a piece of cloth. Then she helps her son into his outdoor clothes and presses the bundle into his hands, and Oskar and Lindgren walk out of the door and onto the gravel path and Oskar turns off in the direction of the woodland half a kilometre from the harbour. They walk there in silence, side by side. Lindgren clutches the bundle to his chest and keeps his eyes firmly on the ground. They head for the woods and Oskar does not have the heart to deny Lindgren his outing with a picnic, even though the fog is swirling and their breath steams around their faces.

♦

Then Oskar sits Lindgren down on a tree stump at the edge of the wood, takes the bundle and after a while manages, in spite of the damp, to start a small sputtering fire and warm the coffee. Then they each sit on a tree stump facing one another in the cold and the silence. Autumn is already well advanced this year.

Lindgren stares dumbly ahead. Oskar looks at him with sadness in his heart. So they sit there in silence on this September woodland outing with a picnic and Oskar then gently asks:

"How are you doing, Lindgren?"

"Very well, thanks. It was ni . . ."

Then his words drown. His brain is able to transmit a first impulse and his nerves can transform this into an opening, but then he is unable to continue the sentence.

So they fall silent once more before Oskar tries again.

"Your mother seems very fit."

"She really is ve . . ."

The words fade away and Lindgren's mouth hangs slack, open.

They sit opposite one another like this for nearly an hour before Oskar packs up the bundle, takes Lindgren by the arm and walks him back home.

♦

When Oskar leaves Lindgren's house it is late in the afternoon and, as he turns onto the quayside, he reflects that today he has been out of work for exactly six months. It was a Sunday like today when he realised that come the Monday he too would be dismissed.

◆

Oskar is forty-four this year. Lindgren, who is now tucked up in the kitchen sofa, is the same age. Oskar is one of thousands who are unemployed. Lindgren has a brain which will soon have ceased to function. They have celebrated a Sunday in September together, as autumn creeps closer and closer.

◆

On Sundays those who have been laid off no longer wear their work clothes, the way they do the rest of the week even though they have no jobs. Every weekday morning, they put on their usual clothes before setting off on the long trek between the State Unemployment Agency, the factory gates, cafés and home. But there are no jobs, because the depression has the nation's whole economy in its grip. Goods lie piled up in warehouses. There are no buyers and the gates remain closed. The public relief work which the State Unemployment Agency organises – wood-chopping, forest clearance, snow-shovelling and foraging for coal – has hundreds of applicants for each opening. And the mass of unemployed grows. The days come and go. National socialists and communists take turns out in the streets. The Social Democrats gradually consolidate their newly acquired position in power.

But on Sundays you get into your best clothes and roam around town and Oskar, who is not yet ready to eat, goes into the café down at the harbour. He walks into the crowded room. He nods at people and some of them nod back at him. He spots an empty place at someone else's table, orders coffee and blows into his hands to warm them. An old railway worker is sitting on the other side of the table. Oskar recognises him from some photographs in the local newspaper. Oskar knows that he is called Leandersson and that he is a relatively successful local wrestler. Leandersson beats nearly everyone in the bantamweight class and, if he were not already nearly forty years old, he could even have had a successful career at a higher level.

Leandersson looks at Oskar and gives a slightly crooked smile. A little curious, Oskar looks for the famous cauliflower ears which wrestlers soon develop. But Leandersson's ears are smooth, without swollen earlobes or damaged cartilage.

Leandersson is drinking beer. In front of him on the table he also has a black notebook. It is greasy and he runs his thumb across the smooth surface.

"Is this seat free?"

"Go on, sit down."

"The weather's pretty rough."

"Autumn's early this year. The houses are cold. And I suppose you're also out of work."

"I am."

"What do you do?"

"I'm a blaster."

"I see. I'm on the railways."

"And a wrestler, right?"

"Well. I could have become one maybe. But I'd say it's too late now."

"I read about you in the papers sometimes."

"I think it's not me who's good but the opposition that's bad. I usually wrap a load of scrap iron in a mattress and train with that. That's about the toughest opposition I get."

"Really? Are there so few who wrestle?"

"That's not it. I'm in the wrong division. There don't seem to be many who weigh as much as I do. Or as little, I suppose I should say."

"I see. But in that case, can't you put on or lose some weight?"

"I don't want to. It's not worth it. At any rate, not any longer."

"How long's it been?"

"Without a job? I've been chopping wood for a mate who was off sick for a few days but apart from that it's been four months, nearly five, I think."

"That's bloody terrible."

"You can say that again."

"And it doesn't seem to be getting any better."

"It probably will, eventually."

"Let's hope so."

"Yes. Let's."

◆

Then Leandersson starts to leaf through his black notebook and Oskar stirs his cup and looks around the café. The warmth and the smoke are getting in his eyes and he asks to pay. Just as he is about to get up and leave, Leandersson slams his notebook shut.

"One can't very well just sit around and do nothing. And I can't wrestle with those bloody mattresses every day."

Oskar, who had been about to go, remains seated.

"No."

"So I've been spending some time tracing my ancestors."

"Is that so?"

"I'm trying to find out where I come from. It's pretty interesting when you find something. I've been looking at church records here and there. Luckily the family comes from villages around here so I can use my bicycle."

"Indeed?"

"I knew that Farfar on my father's side had been a farmer, but I had no idea where his parents came from. But now I know a little more."

Leandersson the wrestler then opens his notebook and begins to read.

"My great-grandfather's name was Leander and he came over from Denmark. He moved here in 1802. He was described as a farmer, but he must have been a sailor as well since it says that he was lost in a storm, was never heard of again and was then declared dead in 1821 at the request of his wife Maria Louisa. Then I've written to a parish in Jutland and they tell me that a Leander emigrated in 1800 and bugger me if he didn't push off on the first day of the century, January 1, taking his wife and a child with him. Farfar wasn't born until later. But in that letter from Jutland it then says that Leander was born in 1769 and that he was the son of somebody called Christian Leander, who was also a farmer, born in 1738. But that's as far as I've got. Now I'm getting to grips with my mother's side. It'll be interesting to see where that leads. I had no bloody clue that there were Danes in the family. But you've got to keep yourself busy with something."

"It's interesting to find out all that."

"Certainly is."

Then Oskar gets up, they nod at each other and Oskar leaves the café.

On the way home he stops at the display window of the newspaper office and looks at the pictures there. He can count as many as eleven in which you see Per Albin Hansson.

◆

On his way out of Parliament. On his way into Parliament.

Patting a cow and smiling at the camera.

Talking to von Sydow.

On a rostrum at the People's House in Sala.

On a rostrum at the People's House in Norrtälje.

On a rostrum at the People's House in Värnamo.

In an armchair in his office.

With his cabinet on the way to a meeting of the government.

With his cabinet on the way back from a meeting of the government.

In his office with a general in attendance.

◆

The window is misted over on the inside and the lighting is poor. Oskar examines the pictures one after the other and counts them twice. Then he goes on his way.

♦

Later they sit at the kitchen table, he and she, and Oskar talks about Lindgren.

"Is it really that bad?"

"I expect he'll die soon. And she's a bit confused now too. But that's understandable."

"Poor things."

"It's awful."

"Can't medicine help?"

"No. It seems it can't be cured. It just spreads and spreads. The head rots."

"That's terrible."

"He probably doesn't notice it himself."

"Thank goodness for that."

"Yes. But it must have been good for him to get some fresh air."

"That must have made her happy."

"Yes. It did."

Then they fall silent and soon they will sleep.

♦

When they have gone to bed, she tells him that in a few days, on September 12, 1932, there is going to be a political debate on the radio. While sleep steals over them, they go on talking.

"Who's taking part?"

"Per Albin. Wigforss."

"What about the other side?"

"Pehrsson. Axel Pehrsson. The bloke who bought the Bramstorp property."

"Why not Sköld? And Engberg?"

"We can't just have our lot, can we?"

"Will they be talking about Kreuger in that case?"

"They've got more important things to discuss, I imagine. Now that we're in government. There are thirty million people around the world who are out of work."

"How do you know?"

"I saw it in the paper."

"But here?"

"There must be more than a hundred thousand without a job."

"Maybe we should be giving them a voice."

"Yes."

◆

Until the end of the 1920s, Oskar has no idea what determines labour and wages, crises and economic booms. He does his job and is only faintly worried at the prospect of becoming one of the 16 per cent of Trade Union Confederation members who are out of work. He listens to discussions, he sees changes, he reads newspapers, but has no understanding of the forces that drive the economic and social situation. He works and is present.

◆

The next day Oskar is sitting in a café in the harbour, listening in on a conversation. Two brothers are sitting at a table by the window. There is no-one else there. That is because an important football match is being played in the town that same day.

The younger brother is a syndicalist. The other is a follower of Kilbom. There is a striking similarity between them. They use the same gestures and have the same halting way of expressing themselves. Oskar is alone at the far end of the room and he hears their increasingly heated conversation. The waitress leans against the counter, scratching her chin.

It is not known what the two brothers said to each other, but when Oskar leaves it is with one thought in mind. He walks fast and the momentum helps to push ahead this idea that has possessed him. When he gets home, he stops abruptly in front of the door and then continues on at the same pace.

He strides four times around the block before entering the house and climbing the two flights of stairs. His thought has now become a clear image inside his head and he is almost elated.

That night, after Elvira has fallen asleep, he goes into the kitchen and sits at the table. He turns to a page in his union passbook and tears it out as delicately as he can. And, after reflecting for a while, he writes in clear block letters:

◆

TOMORROW THERE WILL BE A POLITICAL
DEBATE ON THE RADIO.

WE UNEMPLOYED WORKERS AND SOCIAL
DEMOCRATS MUST LISTEN TO THE THOUGHTS
AND WORDS OF OUR ELECTED LEADERS.

◆

Then he signs it "Oskar". He leaves the piece of paper on the table and steals into the bedroom so as not to wake her up. There he gets dressed and then returns to the kitchen. He picks up the paper and tiptoes out of the front door.

He is alone in the deserted streets and keeps close to the walls of the houses. He walks all the way to the main square and stops for a moment in a doorway. He listens to the deep silence and then hurries over to the glass door of the savings bank. There he fastens the piece of paper that he has torn out of his union passbook. He spits on the back and presses it against the glass.

Then he hurries home. As he comes in through the door he listens for a while to her breathing to be sure that she is asleep. Then he undresses, puts his clothes on a kitchen chair and pulls on his nightshirt. He sits on one of the chairs and smiles to himself. He leafs through his union passbook, from which the page is missing, and it is very late when he gets into his side of the bed to sleep.

◆

But she had not been sleeping. When he went out a few hours earlier she had quickly got dressed and followed him. While he had been standing in the doorway close to the largest square, waiting and listening, she had been in another doorway a little further down the street. When he was by the window she had stopped in the same place as he had a minute or two earlier and was terrified, thinking he was about to commit a crime.

As he leaves the savings bank window she remains where

she is in the doorway. Then she runs up, sees the sheet of paper, reads the text and hurries home across backyards and over boarded fences to get back before him.

She gets into bed fully dressed, with coat and shoes on under the blanket, and hears him come in, hears him pause to make sure she is asleep, sees him undress, sees him sit at the kitchen table and turn the pages of his union passbook, and only once he has got into his side of the bed and she is certain that he is asleep does she slip out from under the bedclothes, avoid the creaking floorboard which is the third one along from the kitchen door, take off her clothes and crawl back under the blanket again.

Only then is she filled with joy, and she lies awake until morning when they get up together and Oskar asks how she has slept.

Then they have their coffee and porridge. They hear the neighbours upstairs begin to argue and eventually Oskar goes up to them to borrow a little sugar, and he knows he has made both of them happy because the arguing stops.

◆

Oskar starts work again in 1933. He is among the first to get a job after unemployment peaks early in the year. In May he begins working in Stockholm and it is there one Sunday that he sees the Nazis parading through the streets. He feels a knot in his stomach as he stands on the pavement and sees them passing and recognises Sergeant Lindholm right at the front. He can imagine himself charging in and jabbing his finger and thumb into the sergeant's face.

Then, after the procession has gone by, Oskar goes back to where he is living, a rented room on Katarina Bangata, and the next day he reads in the newspapers how the Nazis were set upon in Humlegården by some young communists and others.

At a Nazi election rally in early summer he is standing to one side by a tree in a park and listening to the hoarse and strident language in which the speaker clearly states that there are many who will have to go, and Oskar realises that he is one of them.

◆

Later he returns to his home town and once again joins the ranks of the unemployed. He continues to take Lindgren out for walks, but he avoids the woodland where they had their picnic when autumn had already set in. He is the only one in church at Lindgren's funeral, apart from his mother.

When she is about to go home, for the second time the mother holds out her weathered arm, which looks like a stick, and Oskar takes hold of it with his finger and thumb and he is very moved when he sees how confused she is.

◆

The first time Oskar sees Hitler's face is one day in 1936. He and Elvira are standing in front of the window of the newspaper office, looking at pictures from Hinke Bergegren's funeral. She is just saying that she thinks she recognises one of the women in grey coats pulling the funerary carriage, to which he mutters an indistinct "Is that so?", when he sees

Hitler, his hand raised, inspecting serried ranks of young women in a large stadium.

He has come across pictures of Hitler before, but now it is as if he were seeing the face for the first time. The clenched jaw muscles. The low forehead with the deep folds. And as he looks at those young women lined up in rows, he has the impression that he is seeing the face clearly for the first time.

Then they move on and as they pass the savings bank window they are sharing an experience without Oskar being aware of it.

They take their time walking home and speak in low voices, with many steps between their words.

"It's cold."

"Yes."

"Did you remember to pay the rent?"

"I did."

"Are your shoes alright?"

"What do you mean, alright?"

"Are your feet getting wet?"

"They're not too bad."

"The shoes will wear out again, I'm sure."

"Not yet though."

"Let's hope they last."

"There's nothing wrong with the left shoe."

"Funny that only one keeps giving out."

"Yes, it is a bit strange."

◆

And like all the other unemployed they struggle on and in time leave the thirties behind for a war which will last nearly six years. That evening in 1936, Oskar is forty-eight and he walks by her side and looks at the stones on the pavement.

♦

His thoughts rarely went beyond anything to do with his family. It was his joy that they never had to do without any of the necessities of life.

♦

At night he dreamed about the pictures he saw through the steamed-up window of the newspaper office. He dreamed about the day just past. Sometimes he dreamed that he was running with other children and shouting and climbing through holes in the boards between backyards.

He wished for what was in his thoughts and believed in the things that filled his dreams.

♦

One afternoon in 1937 there is a knock at Oskar's door. Once more it is a Sunday. They are sitting at the kitchen table and have just eaten.

When Elvira opens the door, there is a person standing there whom they both recognise. It is a woman, about forty years old, who is one of the driving forces behind an animal welfare association in the town. It is well known. It has been agitating for more humane treatment of various domestic animals. She is married to an engineer at the largest textile factory, where Elvira once worked.

"I hope I'm not disturbing. Good afternoon."

"Please, come in."

"Thank you. I'm here to ask you for a little help, Herr Johansson. As you may know, I belong to a group which is actively engaged in trying to improve the lot of our most common pets, above all cats and dogs."

◆

The visitor speaks with passion, barely pausing for breath. She sits on the edge of a kitchen chair. Oskar is in the sofa. Elvira stands by the window.

◆

"The thing is that we're planning to put on an amateur show at Easter where we'd promote awareness of our activities and also have a sale of home-made articles and handicrafts donated by active members or supporters of our organisation or produced during our weekly get-togethers. And you see we're thinking of having one scene in which we compare the injuries that irresponsible people inflict on their pets with those which human beings themselves can suffer. Now you, Herr Johansson, once had a serious accident which luckily ended well. We thought that one could compare the assistance you yourself received with the help that animals don't get. It may seem a little far-fetched and odd, but we know that the only way people can be made to realise how badly they treat their pets is to contrast their treatment with their own situation. We were thinking of a scene in which a cat suffers an accident and is then dumped on a rubbish heap and after that we'd have another one in which you, Herr Johansson, have your blasting accident and then all the doctors and the whole hospital manage to save your life."

◆

After this torrent, she suddenly stops. When Oskar realises that she is waiting for an answer, he cannot utter a single word. And she is able to continue.

◆

"You wouldn't actually be acting out the scenes themselves, Herr Johansson, you'd only come in right at the end and hold a cat in your arms. Then you would just stand on stage for a moment before the curtain falls.

"We would of course be very grateful if you could help us with this, Herr Johansson. We obviously wouldn't be able to pay you, but it is for the worthiest of causes."

"Yes."

"I know that you won't say no."

"No."

Oskar sits in the kitchen sofa, Elvira stands by the window and ten minutes later it is agreed.

For the two rehearsals, Oskar has a wastepaper basket in his arms. The first time he enters from the right and stands in the spotlight in the middle of the stage for eleven minutes, because something has gone wrong with the curtain ropes.

The second time he stands with his wastepaper basket for three minutes and everything runs smoothly.

During the first night and the three other performances, Oskar makes his entrance with a neutered tomcat which is black apart from a mark on its forehead. The cat is heavy and Oskar clutches it to his stomach. As Oskar goes onstage he is blinded by the light and notices that everything is very quiet. When the curtain is drawn shut and the light is dimmed, he leaves the stage and puts the cat down in a brown basket. Then he sits backstage on a broken ladder for more than an hour and a half. After that he goes back on for the curtain call with all the other actors.

◆

Elvira sees the last performance. As they are lying in bed that night, she says that the whole thing was quite good but that Oskar looked dreadful in the harsh spotlight. Never before had she realised how badly injured his face was. Then she asks if the cat was heavy because that is how it seemed and Oskar answers that it weighed as much as a sledgehammer and then they fall asleep. First Oskar. Then she.

◆

At Christmas that year a letter arrives from the animal welfare association. They thank Oskar for his participation and inform him that the collection, together with the proceeds from the sale of handicrafts, had amounted to 495 kronor and 34 öre, which has to be considered a success.

◆

Some time later, Elvira asks what the cat's name was. Oskar
cannot remember but he says that it was called Nisse.

The Poster

In early April in 1949, Oskar buys a propaganda poster. It is one of the most famous ones, the most widely disseminated and translated, but above all perhaps the most effective graphic analysis of the capitalist system ever published. It is the well-known pyramid, which was first printed in the U.S.A. in about 1910.

The poster shows the pyramid on different levels, open on all sides. Right at the top is a sack full of money with four dollar signs on it, drawn like an illustration from a children's storybook. On the next level below, where the pyramid starts to widen, three people are crowded together. The middle one is a king, dressed like the king on a playing card, or in a fairy tale. He is flanked by two heads of state wearing tailcoats and holding top hats. The next level down shows three priests. One Greek Orthodox, one Catholic and one Lutheran. They are standing far apart and do not seem to be relating to each other in any way. The Greek Orthodox priest is holding up his cross and turned towards the right. The Lutheran is in the middle and looks straight ahead. The Catholic priest is facing to the left. In the picture, they all have open mouths.

On the next level, exactly halfway down the pyramid, are the armed forces. Two cannon, their barrels pointed diagonally outwards, an officer with sabre raised and two regular soldiers frozen in an attacking pose. The services represented are the infantry and artillery and they are wearing American uniforms. At the rear of this image and the two previous ones are Gothic pillars supporting the platforms. The backdrop consists of large glass windows.

The next level, the second-widest and penultimate one, represents a large dining table, where rich bourgeois sit together, glasses raised, and they have turned as if to greet the person looking at the poster. They are all in high spirits, but one has fallen asleep on the table. The tablecloth is messy and the whole scene gives the impression of unrestrained gluttony.

And then the bottom level, the base that holds up the whole pyramid. There you have the workers, bearing everything on their shoulders. Industrial workers, blacksmiths, children, women, farmers and old people crowded together. There is a tremendous sense of concentrated power in the picture. To the left side you can see a red flag, flapping violently. The people nearest the flag have their eyes raised to the levels above. One is looking at the military and clenches his fist. Another looks at the dining table. A third, a woman, can just make out the feet of the diners. But none of them sees higher than that. In the front, to the right of the picture, is a child lying down. It is not hard to see that it is starved, perhaps dead. Further over stands a man who is lifting a shovel. He looks up at the pyramid, but it is difficult to say what exactly he has fixed his eyes upon.

•

Oskar buys the poster and pins it up in the kitchen. The text is in English, but the image is too clear for him to need to understand what it says.

◆

> We rule you, We fool you, We shoot at you,
> We eat for you, We work for all – and finally
> We feed all.

◆

Often they sit and look at the poster. Not just because they spend a lot of time in the kitchen every day and the poster is there on the wall above the kitchen sofa and it is hard not to see it. They sit and they look at it and every time they notice something new, some new detail, some new combination. And the illustrations provoke thoughts and discussions. The propaganda poster becomes a textbook, because that is how they use it. At the same time, it represents a challenge and a call to action. That is the meaning Elvira reads into it one day and she says that she feels it would only take one more person to stand underneath the bottom level for there to be enough power to topple the whole pyramid and bring it to the ground. Then they sit for a long time and laugh and talk about the chaos that would ensue. How the one who had fallen asleep at the dining table would have a shock when he woke up. How bottles and glasses would be smashed over the priests and the soldiers. How the cannon would explode and tear apart the sack of money. How the skirts of the female diners would ride all the way up their thighs and how those who had propped up the pyramid for so long would be able to stretch their shoulders and their backs.

"Imagine all the cracking when everyone straightens out their backs. It would sound like thunder."

But their one persistent thought about the poster is the feeling that those who are sustaining the whole structure seem so amazingly real to them. Once, when Oskar is lying in bed, he says that they are out there in the kitchen, supporting and supporting and supporting.

◆

On April 24, 1949 the Social Democrats celebrate their sixtieth anniversary. A large celebration is held in the Stockholm Concert Hall. August Söderman's "Swedish Festival Music" is performed on a stage filled with flowers. The festivities reach a climax during the demonstrations on May 1, which are entirely given over to the anniversary.

Oskar and Elvira get up early. They set out at half past eight and it is warm and still. They leave the town and follow a gravel path into the forest. Once they are under the trees, in the shade, it is cooler and they walk side by side, quickly, to keep themselves warm. The ground is dry and there is a crackling underfoot. They walk in silence and follow the gravel path up the gently sloping ridge, for four kilometres, until the path merges into a clear-cut in the wood. There are three large stacks of stripped and unsorted pinewood there. The air is heavy with the smell of resin and they lean against one of the piles, careful not to get their clothes sticky. Then they close their eyes and turn towards the sun.

They stand there for a long time, silent and with their eyes shut, listening to the sighing of the forest.

◆

In the afternoon they join the march, in the last third of the procession. The demonstrators are walking six abreast and both Oskar and Elvira are singing along. During the course of the demonstration they sing all the verses of the Internationale twice over and hum along to the tune of "The Sons of Labour". Both take care to stay in their line of six and all the time they make sure to keep in step.

In the People's Park the local chairman, a sixty-year-old metalworker, makes a speech. He sticks to the topic of the jubilee throughout and quotes each of Axel Danielsson, Branting and Ernst Wigforss. The only specifically political questions he raises are to do with house construction and the continued and expanded building of homes for the elderly. He talks about collective laundries and closes with a mention of the congress that same autumn in London, which will establish the International Confederation of Free Trade Unions.

He is speaking from the bandstand and has a strong voice. Oskar and Elvira are almost at the front by the podium, and standing there motionless and looking up and taking in every word.

That evening, as they sit in the kitchen and talk about the demonstration, Oskar suddenly points at the poster on the wall.

"But if you look at this picture, compare it to our situation today, you can see how little is being achieved."

"You can't say that, surely."

"I can. Because in some strange way it's as if what is happening is that some of those standing and bearing the weight down at the bottom suddenly get to climb up to the dining table, while their place as bearers is taken by some others. And then it's as if those at the top, the kings and the priests, are leaning forward and showing their faces, so that those down there, who are holding it all up, can see them. But the pyramid is still a pyramid. I mean, those doing the supporting get new clothes, eat different food, but they're still left way down there, waving their flags, and those up at the top are still right up there."

"But it's not as though they can still do whatever they want."

"Agreed, but all the same they're still up there at the top."

"How do you mean, up there?"

"Well. They don't earn any less just because we get a bit more. And they don't get to decide any less just because we decide more, if indeed we do."

"But how would the government get anything done then? And they genuinely do."

"I don't know. But the ones up there are up there. Where would we be standing in the picture?"

"Down at the bottom, where else?"

"For how long?"

"It takes time. These things don't happen overnight. One can't expect that."

"No. I understand that."

"Don't you believe me?"

"The point isn't whether I believe you or not, is it? It's how things are."

"Yes."

"And that is the way it is."

"What do you mean?"

"That the ones up there are up there. And we're here. Standing at the bottom and raising our heads up behind the sofa."

"Surely not everyone hangs their poster behind a sofa?"

"No."

"I'm not sure I really understand what you mean."

"What I mean is, the only thing that's really happened is that now we see things for what they are. Other than that, nothing has changed."

"I don't agree. Just look at how we live!"

"Fair enough. But a pyramid which reflects the situation in Sweden today wouldn't look any different. It simply wouldn't. Just slightly different clothes. And planes instead of cannon."

"They've still got cannon, haven't they?"

"These days it's more and more planes."

"That doesn't make it any better."

"No. But the pyramid is still the same and that was printed in 1911. It says so down in the corner."

"I've seen that."

"So something's wrong. And things are not exactly moving fast."

"Obviously not."

"Is that so obvious? It feels as if it's all slowing down."

"What should we do, then?"

"Become communists, maybe."

"Will that make it happen any faster?"

"It should do. They're more direct, after all."

"But there aren't enough of them."

"That can change."

"I don't think it will."

"But it might well."

◆

And the poster seems so real to them, and Oskar looks at those who support and support and support.

◆

"Domö ought to have that poster."

"The conservative leader? Why?"

"It wouldn't do any harm."

"You think so?"

"Yes."

"But he's stepping down now, isn't he?"

"Is he?"

"I think so. I read it somewhere."

"Who's replacing him?"

"I don't know. Maybe they don't even know themselves."

"No. Maybe not."

Then they go to bed and the poster hangs over the sofa.

◆

One night, one of the yellow drawing pins in the right-hand corner of the poster comes loose. When Oskar sees it in the morning, he thinks that at least this pyramid has finally collapsed. To see if Elvira notices, he turns it upside down on the wall. She only sees it that evening and they laugh and they put it back the right way up together.

·

Oskar is now sixty-one years old. He is starting to feel tired in the mornings and on Sundays he likes to sleep until eleven. From time to time he thinks he may be ill, but he never goes and gets himself examined. Sometimes the two of them will sit and talk about the fact that they are getting old and then occasionally they both feel very frightened at the thought of being left alone. They never say so to each other, but each is gripped by a sudden anxiety that they will be the one who survives the other. Both of them harbour this fear, which grows stronger and more pervasive with each passing day. But they never speak of it. Only rarely do they talk about old age.

·

At the same time, around 1950, Oskar increasingly longs to spend more time in the countryside. His thoughts are not detailed or clear-cut but there is always water in the scenes of nature he conjures up in his mind. They vary between small rivers and the seashore, forest lakes and torrents. But the water is always there, without his knowing exactly why.

And as his thoughts begin to dwell on nature and water, he also feels hopeful that he will live to a great age.

·

He does not know why, but one day he is suddenly certain that he will be allowed to grow old. And it makes him happy and the images of nature crop up in his mind increasingly often.

But on Sundays he prefers to sleep rather than go out. He lies in his bed and sees the images in his mind. Only on rare occasions, such as on the first day of May, do they go out into the forest.

◆

One Thursday, Oskar is asked if he would like to stop working and retire. He is surprised, but after a few seconds he answers with an emphatic no.

"No. Not yet, not unless I have to."

And just once, that same evening as he is sitting on a chair in the kitchen, untying one of his shoelaces, he stops what he is doing and thinks that it might have been nice after all.

But he wants to go on working for a few more years. And he feels deep inside that if he were not so sure that he would live to become old, then he would stop work as soon as he could.

The Developing Process in Photography

One day in August in 1958, Oskar is sitting by his radio, listening to Lennart Hyland report on the unbelievable atmosphere as Richard Dahl skims over the bar at 2.12 metres. He only just clears it and the bar trembles and for a few seconds there is total silence on this day during the European Championships. But once it is clear that the bar will not fall, a fearsome racket breaks out in the Stockholm Olympic Stadium and Oskar can hear his neighbours in the upstairs apartment stamp on the floor and bang their fists on the table. Oskar feels his heart pounding inside his ribs and he is overwhelmed with joy that Richard Dahl has surpassed himself. It does not cross his mind that this means a gold medal for Sweden, and likely the only one. Then he gets up and measures out a rough 212 centimetres on one wall of the kitchen. He is amazed when he sees the result.

◆

In the course of 1958, Oskar has read a lot about sport in the newspapers and listened to a great deal on the radio. Many reports said that it was unlikely this century would ever again see such a year for sporting events in Sweden. There were the European athletics championships and a football World

Cup with Sweden as the runners-up, and Oskar once saw the left-back Sven Axbom in the street.

But Oskar is not particularly interested. Sometimes he is enthralled by the atmosphere, by success and adversity, but often he does not even know the rules of the different sports. He is also capable of laughing at himself, like the time when he realises that relay races do not work as he had thought: which was that the runners turn around and sprint back again at every baton handover.

One of the first World Cup matches is between Sweden and Hungary. It is an evenly poised and exciting game with Sweden leading 2–1 in the middle of the second half. Then the Hungarians start to apply more pressure and begin to dominate. Lennart Hyland gets excited. After the Hungarians have laid siege to the Swedish goal for a long time, their inside left aims a hard and well-placed shot at goal with his instep. Kalle Svensson has to stretch as far as he can to tip the ball around the right-hand goalpost. Just as the Hungarians get ready to take their corner and Oskar is on tenterhooks, he clamps his jaws shut and feels one of his upper canines crumble . . . He sticks his thumb into his mouth and pushes half of the tooth out onto the tablecloth. He feels a shooting pain and realises that the nerve is exposed.

◆

The next day he goes to a dentist, who knocks out the rest of the tooth and kills the nerve. At the same time, he examines Oskar's other teeth and after a while says that Oskar's teeth are coming loose in both his upper and lower jaws and that the condition is too far advanced for it to be corrected without surgery. The dentist tells him what that would cost and Oskar replies that it is impossible. When he then asks how long he is likely to keep his teeth, the dentist answers that in all likelihood he will lose them quite quickly. Then, when Oskar leaves, he is given a brochure which describes what it is like to have dentures. Oskar sits down at the kitchen table and studies the brochure intently. He tries to imagine wearing a dental plate and feels uncomfortable at the thought. He puts aside the brochure and knows that he will never wear false teeth. He would rather go toothless. For the rest of the day he feels very unhappy at the thought that his body is starting to fall apart.

That evening he gets undressed, pulls the kitchen curtains shut and sits naked on a chair in the middle of the room. Then he carefully examines his body. He pinches his skin, scratches it with the nail of his index finger. He stretches and clenches his toes and tries to bend in different directions. He checks his pulse on his carotid artery. He blocks one ear at a time while he listens for sounds from the apartments next door.

When he has finished his examination, he realises to his surprise that he has been sitting naked on the chair for more than an hour. He finds it hard to believe that so much time has passed. He puts on his nightshirt and goes to bed. He lies there with his mental images and on this particular evening he sees a greenish-blue ocean which is perfectly calm, and he tries to conjure up a string of memories. He falls asleep picturing all this.

♦

A few years earlier a total eclipse of the sun was visible in the country. There is great excitement, because it is not going to recur in the foreseeable future. It has therefore been turned into a sacred moment, lasting less than a minute. Like everybody else, Oskar prepares himself for the day. Well in advance he makes sure that he has a piece of blackened glass through which he can watch the moon's disc gliding in front of the sun. With growing interest, he follows the discussions of the meteorologists as to whether the eclipse will take place behind thick cloud cover or whether it will be possible to see it.

He is out early that morning. He puts the blackened glass, which he has wrapped in a handkerchief, in his pocket and follows the gravel path out into the forest. Walking along, he thinks back to the times he has gone there with Elvira. The thought makes him a little melancholy, but at the same time he is happy that he is still alive and can experience the remarkable eclipse. He stops in the clear-cut and sees that there are only very few clouds gliding across the sky. He has put an alarm clock in his other pocket and has set it by the radio. He puts it on a tree stump and finds himself a low pile of logs to sit on. The air is warm and he squints at the sun.

Then he stays sitting on the woodpile, alone, as he waits for the momentous occasion.

He keeps an eye on the hands of the clock and stands up as the time approaches. He has set the clock to go off a quarter of an hour before the eclipse is due. He hears it and sees a squirrel stop in surprise halfway up the trunk of a pine tree. He unwraps the blackened glass from the handkerchief and with his head tilted upwards he holds the glass before his eye.

There he stands, following the whole eclipse with a slight shudder as the bright day turns to dark. He does not move a muscle and can hear the clock ticking beside him.

◆

When it is all over and he packs up his handkerchief, the blackened glass and the alarm clock, he feels happy to have been able to experience this extraordinary event. He walks the gravel path back to town, thinking that at that very instant of total eclipse, time no longer ran on and away, instead it increased and expanded sideways. And he thinks that he would like time to be like that always. But he also thinks that it is not possible and, when he gets home, he drops the blackened glass and the dirty handkerchief into the rubbish bin in the yard.

◆

One day, a year later, the local newspaper carries a detailed description of how photographs are developed. Oskar reads the article several times before he puts it to one side on the table.

Then he reflects that his thoughts and dreams are just like the process he has recently read about for developing photographs. The way the negative, which is sharp but has no detail, slowly transforms into an ample and faithful representation of a moment and a situation and perhaps also a mood. That is exactly how he believes his brain functions, and he tears out the article and puts it in the drawer of the kitchen table.

◆

During the fifties, four main events influence Oskar's political stance. And three of them are also important and decisive developments during that decade, which people so wrongly see as somewhat static, a political vacuum compared to the sixties or the forties. Those three events are the atom bomb and the discussion as to whether Sweden should have such weapons, the uprising in Hungary in 1956 and the Suez crisis. The fourth event is Oskar's experience of how a high-rise development takes shape in the neighbourhood from which he is forced to move in December 1959.

◆

The atom bomb frightened Oskar. When he read about the vast numbers of victims claimed by each of the bombs and about the stockpiling the great powers were already engaged in, he felt a fear that was almost panic. Oskar only read the local press, but the other newspapers were often quoted there and he followed the debate with a growing sense of despondency combined with an increasingly strong disapproval of what the political parties were doing. Oskar read Tingsten's words, which were cited in the newspapers. He was briefly cheered by Östen Undén's relatively strong pronouncement against nuclear weapons, but he still thought that it was insufficient.

Then there was a minor event that instilled a lasting fear in Oskar. It was when he saw an article about the two bombs which were dropped on Bikini Atoll in the summer of 1946. Nearly fifteen years had passed when he reads the article and learns that the two atom bombs had been called by girls' names.

He never forgot this and it fostered in him a strong distrust of America, which would be further magnified by the Vietnam war.

In the end, the question of the atom bomb also alienated Oskar once and for all from the Social Democratic Party. When he left, he was sad that it had to happen, but there was no turning back and he signed up as a member of the new party.

◆

The Hungarian uprising came as a shock to Oskar. When he read about the tanks on the streets of Budapest, and about the fierce battle, and when he listened to the agitated voices giving terrifying reports of the brutal assault, he became completely desperate. He would turn the radio off, only to switch it on again seconds later. He would get to his feet, open a window, go back to the radio and then jump to his feet again to close the window.

◆

The Suez crisis was another major factor in changing his political views. He never altogether understands the causes of this war, but he is deeply affected by the accounts of the suffering endured by the civilian population.

◆

At the end of the fifties, the neighbourhood in which Oskar lives is to be torn down to make way for large high-rise buildings. This is the fourth and perhaps most important event for Oskar during the decade.

One afternoon, when he has gone down to the backyard with rubbish wrapped in a newspaper, the bin has been moved out into the middle of the yard. There are two men taking readings and measurements where it would normally stand. Oskar pauses for a while, hesitating, before dropping his packet of rubbish into the bin, even though it is not where it should be. Then he goes up to the two men and asks what they are doing.

"It's just some calculations for the new housing that's going up."

"Are they building new houses here?"

"Yes, both blocks are going, Nypan and this one, Smeden."

"First I've heard of it."

"The plans haven't been finalised yet. So far, it's only a decision."

"What do you mean, a decision?"

"That there's housing going up here."

"What about us?"

"What do you mean?"

"Those of us who live here."

"I expect they'll make other housing available for you. But

we don't know anything about that. The town owns these blocks, so it's up to them to tell the tenants what will be happening to them."

As Oskar goes back up the stairs he is dumbfounded and walks slowly.

◆

Two months later he gets his notice to move, together with the information that there will be accommodation for him in a rental block in a suburb three kilometres outside town. The letter tells him that he is to move out by September 30 that same year. He is also asked to contact Herr Evertsson in the town's property department for further details.

At the property office, Oskar has to wait forty minutes for Evertsson to arrive. He looks at Oskar for a long time before asking him into his office. He leaves the door to the corridor open and sits down behind the desk.

"It hasn't been all that hard to arrange new accommodation for you, Herr Johansson. We've assumed that you would like to have an apartment approximately the same size as the one you have now."

"I don't want to move."

"I don't think anyone does. But surely we must welcome the fact that housing construction has now finally got going. And of course quality enhancement is also important. Especially for families with small children, for example."

"Do they have to be built just where I live?"

"The town has decided that it is a suitable area. Not least because of the very central location."

"Quite so. That's exactly why I want to stay."

Then Oskar is on the point of saying that he is disabled, but he keeps quiet.

"You'll be given a moving allowance."

"But what about the rent?"

"It hasn't been set for next year yet, but it will obviously have to be a little bit higher, bearing in mind the standard of the new housing."

"How does one get there?"

"Bus routes are being planned."

"I see."

"Right. Do you have any other questions, Herr Johansson?"

"What will the houses look like?"

"Plans and sketches will be on display in the entrance area of the town hall a few weeks from now. Those will give an overview of the whole area, including the individual apartments."

"I see."

"So you're welcome to go and take a look."

"I see."

◆

When Oskar arrives in the entrance hall, it is deserted. He crosses the stone floor, sees a number of sketches pinned to some wooden boards in the darkest corner of the large hall. He goes up to the boards and notices right away that there are no proper pictures showing what the housing area is going to look like. Only architectural drawings and various cost calculations. Behind him he hears steps echoing in distant corridors, tapping against the stone floors. He pauses and looks at the abstract and incomprehensible drawings. He sees the black lines running into and out of each other like labyrinths. He sees numbers with strange symbols between them.

At that moment Oskar feels he has been tricked and he becomes furious. He looks around and unfastens one of the drawings and turns it upside down. Then he takes a pen out of his pocket and adds a nought and a number here and there to the various calculations. He takes great pains to make the figures look as credible as possible and does not stop until he is satisfied.

Then he leaves.

◆

A few days later he reads in the local newspaper that a somewhat unfortunate incident has occurred in connection with a study group visiting from Finland. The Finnish guests were being escorted through the town hall by one of the town architects, and when they were taken to see the drawings of the new Hamnborgen neighbourhood in the entrance hall, the architect guiding the party discovered that one of the sketches had been turned upside down. This was swiftly put right. It is thought that this was evidence of some visitor's peculiar sense of humour. The town's property department does not deem it necessary to take any measures other than to have a caretaker come to check the drawings at regular intervals.

For several days afterwards, Oskar searches the morning newspaper for confirmation that they have also discovered his sabotage of the calculations. But there is nothing there and one day Oskar goes to the town hall and finds that the drawings have gone and have been replaced by an exhibition of photographs of the newly inaugurated town library.

◆

The matter of Oskar's rearranged figures, which nobody had discovered, becomes one of decisive importance to him. It brings home to him the tremendous extent of arbitrary power that technical people and civil servants have managed to acquire. He is disgusted by the self-importance of these people. He knows that most of them owe their careers to their Social Democratic Party membership. And he no longer wants any part of that.

◆

During these years in the late fifties, when he has become a widower, Oskar rarely talks to anybody. He keeps in touch with his children, but he has no social life and feels no need for one either. He experiences silence as a spacious and cosy place in which to think, dream and conjure up images of nature. He establishes a simple and effective routine for himself and that suits him.

◆

On New Year's Eve 1959, he is standing by a window which

he has opened. It is cold outside and he stands there, looking out at the town from his apartment on the fourth floor of the building he has been forced to move into. In the distance he hears the clocks in the town's three churches strike midnight. Then people start firing off rockets from the balcony below his, so he closes the window and sits down in the kitchen. He has taped the poster onto the wall above the sofa. He sits still and listens to the noises that resonate through the water pipes and from the floor and the ceiling and two of the walls. Where he used to live, you could also hear every sound. But now the noises that come through the concrete seem colder and more invasive and above all more negative. Sometimes he feels like an eavesdropper, somebody who hears but who should not really be doing so. He never had that feeling in his old apartment. There it was simply accepted that the walls were not soundproof and you would act accordingly. In this new building, which is supposed to keep out all noise, the sounds become menacing and alien.

He lives on the fourth floor and does not know his neighbours and is unhappy there. He spends all his time trying to swap his apartment for one in town.

He has been living in the building at Tornvägen 9d for one and a half years, when one day his son comes out and tells him that he knows of a place in town which his father could have. Oskar makes up his mind without even seeing the apartment and one month later he has moved in and it becomes his last-ever home. He will live there until he dies and from early spring till late autumn he moves out to his cabin in the archipelago.

♦

Thus was Oskar ushered into the sixties, carrying with him from the fifties his new solitude and his new party allegiance. But what mattered most to him was that his longing for nature and the sea had now been satisfied.

♦

And all along he held on to this conviction, this faith in his own role, that he had never been nor ever would be anything extraordinary but, rather, was someone who at some point at the end of the last century had played the same games as other children. He had run and yelled and shouted, clambered over boards between backyards, and all the time, throughout his life, he keeps coming back to this perception of himself. He sees it as both the starting point and the sum-total of his life. Neither does he feel that he is missing anything. Once his longing for the sea was satisfied, he was content.

But he went on following all the social changes and maintained that he had been present for them but had not played any role in their coming about. He never denied responsibility or claimed to be free from blame, but neither did he place any value on the role he had played, not even in specific instances in which he had taken a part. He had lived and worked and held his opinions, switched his party allegiance, and deep down inside had his hopes and dreams.

♦

As the years go by, the poster becomes ever more tattered and one day there are so many holes in the corners from all the drawing pins that it falls to the floor. Oskar then rolls it up and ties a piece of string around it. He puts it on a shelf in a wardrobe and never takes it out again.

◆

Oskar lives on with his thoughts and dreams, which he likens to the process for developing photographs.

In One Single Blast,
And Give Them My Regards

Harstena, 3. Clear to moderate visibility.

"That's spot on, that is . . ."

Oskar presses down the button on the transistor radio.

"I need new batteries. Can you get some?"

"Of course."

♦

It is the middle of May. Spring 1966.

♦

"Elvira was a waitress all the time we were together. And always at the same place. You've probably seen it. It's a café down by the railway. For ten years it was called the Barrel. Then there was a change of owner. He bought three new tables and decided to call it Café Paradise. We had a good laugh at that. I think that was the time Elvira liked the least. The proprietor wanted to turn the place into something fancier. He hoped to get rid of the old boys drinking beer and have different customers. But then nobody came at all. He sold up and another owner came along. That was after only three years, just before the war. He bought new chairs and called the place the Barrel again. Elvira liked it there. She knew the old men and what they liked to drink. Mostly beer. Coffee and sandwiches. They opened early, you see. At six o'clock, to serve breakfast. So Elvira got up at five all her life. She went on working when we had the kids. She never took time off. She brought the children along when they were small and they spent the day in the office behind the kitchen. Nobody objected.

"But Elvira went to bed early so as not to tire herself out. As she got older, she would turn in at nine. I stayed up a little while longer. She liked her job very much. The pay was always bad in a job like that, but she got on well with the old boys. She worked from 1919 until she died. One day she burst into tears while we were having supper. I asked her what was wrong and she told me. That her eyesight had got a lot worse in just a few weeks. We went to see the doctor and he said that she had cataracts in both eyes. He would treat her, but it was hard to know. It didn't get any better, but it didn't get worse either. The days before she died, she could see nothing at all, but then there were other reasons for that. The stroke. Up until then she had never been sick in all her life. She laughed a lot and the old blokes liked her. Many of my mates from work went to that café and they always said how good she was. She didn't care if someone got a bit drunk sometimes and if anybody got out of hand she would just drag him out. She wasn't afraid.

"Last winter the café shut down and I believe they've now turned it into a pub. Where you play darts and drink beer.

"The café was closed on Sundays so on the Saturday we would sit up a bit later. We never went out. We were happy at home. It seemed obvious, while the kids were still living with us. We used to sit and have our tea and listen to the radio before there was T.V. They had family programmes like '20 Frågor' and 'Snurran'. Sometimes there was some detective story. And then we got T.V. Every now and then on a Sunday I'd go to watch football with my boy. He was keen. Still is. I never really cared for it, but I went for his sake.

"As they were growing older, the kids started to go out and we'd be sitting up waiting for them to come home. But none of them ever got into trouble. Elvira and I often said so to each other. We were grateful for that.

"When Elvira passed away, my life became very lonely. I tried to keep everything as it was before. I still looked after the flowers, I watered them, but somehow it felt wrong. I didn't change anything. When I'm out here a neighbour does the watering.

"Neither of us ever believed in God. I suppose we were afraid of him when we were children, like everyone else in those days. But when we became socialists, God disappeared. We had a priest for Elvira's funeral, but that was different. None of our children was confirmed. I'm sure they wanted to be. They liked the idea of the presents, same as the others. But we said no. They didn't go to Sunday school either. On the other hand, they all joined the scouts. They thought that was fun.

"Now in the winters I mostly play Patience and watch T.V. There are plenty of good programmes. Sometimes I watch all evening long and have the feeling that I'm learning. Last winter I also switched it on during the mornings, for the school programmes. I enjoyed picking things up.

"I once found an English book in the rubbish room. I tried to read it, but I didn't manage.

"As we grow old it's easy to envy the younger generation. We want to live, let's face it, and be part of it all. Many who complain about young people probably do it because they wish they too were young again. You have to sympathise with that. It's natural. Nobody wants to get old and be put out to grass with gammy legs and a heart turning somersaults in your chest. There's an old couple living on the floor above me. They have jars of medicine standing in every room in case they get taken sick in the kitchen or bathroom. They never go out. They were missionaries in Africa. I've never spoken to them. In the olden days, the elderly were neglected by society. Now they're neglected by both society and their families. It's bad to grow old. But people have always been growing old.

"I'm actually very scared of dying. Especially at night before I go to sleep. Then I sometimes get the idea that I'm never going to wake up again and it's horrible. But when I wake up in the morning, it's no longer on my mind. When I was twenty, I used to believe that there was nothing after death.

"Nothing. We turn into earth and grass. Ten years later, I thought there might be something else. And then I was persuaded that we're born again as another person. It's been changing the whole time. Right now, I'm thinking that living isn't so fantastic that one would want to do it all again. But that too may change, of course. And then I have the children and somehow one lives on through them.

"Elvira and I only ever went on one single trip. It was in 1950.

"It was a coach trip to Austria. I don't know why we went. It just happened somehow. We were to be away two weeks in June. Elvira and I were the only two who were working class. The others were different. We didn't mix with anyone. But it was nice to get out that once. You could still see the signs of war and people were very poor. I think we gave away most of our spending money to beggars. In Vienna we visited a palace which was beautiful. We went and ate out and had a good time. Elvira wasn't afraid. Neither of us understood the language, of course, but she could always explain what we wanted. And she laughed all the time. We bought lots of postcards during the trip. Elvira also made notes in a diary. After she died, I was going through some drawers and found the diary and the cards. I read the notes. Then I threw away the lot of them. It was just too painful to keep it all. It felt sad. The only thing I still have is a photograph of Elvira and me standing in front of a church somewhere in Germany. A photographer took it and said he'd send it to us. We paid in advance and we must have thought we'd never get it. But it arrived in the autumn. It was good of him not to cheat us. The picture is starting to look a bit funny now. It's beginning to fade. But I've still got it. What I remember from the trip is how tough people's lives were. Let's hope there were some socialists down there too.

"Apart from that we never went anywhere. We couldn't afford it."

◆

"Even though both of us worked, all our money was spent on the children. We wanted them to have everything they needed. Elvira once said that what the two of us earned in one month was only half of what many mediocre singers were paid for an evening in an amusement park. It made both of us angry. But by then we were old. Had we been young I'm sure we would have kept up the struggle.

"The Social Democrats' greatest outrage was to have turned socialism into some sort of organisation for unnecessary civil servants to line their pockets at the expense of the workers. There's a way into this society and a way out, but no-one knows what there is in between.

"It's all gone wrong. Terribly wrong. And it can't be put right. Young people have realised that, and therefore I'm confident that sooner or later they'll introduce socialism. Or it may come from outside. It's become clear that what's happening in the rest of the world will force change to happen here too. It's inevitable. Every time there's a revolution somewhere, it makes me happy. Then I sometimes lie on my bed and dream that I'm a part of it. And in some way I am too, obviously."

◆

In 1962 Oskar writes a letter to one of the local newspapers. He argues for pensioners getting a higher state pension so that they can lead a decent life. The letter is clear and concise. Oskar sets out his name and address underneath. He is one of the few to do so. That day he is the only one.

◆

"Once I went into a bookshop and bought a map of the world. I sat for many days looking at all the countries, one by one. It turned out that there were several I'd never heard of. Since then, I always have it in front of me when I watch T.V.

"I've read Moberg's books. They're good. They're like history books, only more exciting. Absolutely gripping. His characters were not in any way remarkable. They were like all the others. But you get to see how much happened in their lives. There ought to be more books like those. Throughout all the centuries, ordinary people have only been allowed to speak in murmurs, yet they were the ones doing all the fighting and being beaten. More ought to be written about things that folk have only been able to talk about in murmurs."

The Lansen jet fighter flies low overhead. The words are drowned out and Oskar falls silent.

◆

"I once took part in a T.V. show. I was in the audience. There were about fifty of us. It was one of the 'Forum' current affairs programmes. But I got angry when they said we could laugh if anyone said something funny. I don't want to be treated like that. Later my boy told me there'd been a close-up of me where you could see my injuries. The eye and the arm. I suppose that can happen."

◆

"I don't like that my boy started to call himself a director as soon as he'd bought a washing machine and started doing people's laundry. The old washerwomen never bloody well called themselves directors, even though they used to have to stand and wash clothes their whole lives. And what about those who clean up other people's shit? The very word makes me angry. Now he has a large laundry business, but he still shouldn't be calling himself a director. I've told him so, but he just laughs. I'm disappointed in him. For a while when he was twenty he was really good and angry and stirred things up. And now he's the sort of person who votes blue. Bloody terrible. It feels as if he's betrayed everything. But it's hard not to love one's children. About once a year I tell him what I really think. He only laughs, though.

"He's got a big house and boats and cars. He's worked for it, of course, but in some way it still feels as if he'd been given it for free. You can see how society has gone off the rails.

"I think things can only be changed through revolution. And it'll come. Sooner or later. But it would have been nice to have been a part of it."

◆

Military manoeuvres are taking place in the archipelago. One morning, Oskar and I see a semi-submerged submarine passing the island.

◆

"Elvira and I were always happy together. We used to lie in bed and chat afterwards. We were constantly tired, but we still managed it a couple of times a week. After we married, neither of us slept with anyone else. I don't think either of us ever needed it. And you're not going to risk something valuable by getting yourself into a stupid mess. So we used to lie there and talk about how things were back then. Elvira would reminisce and so would I. We were never bored. And we spoke about the way things are now and had very much the same views. Elvira was active in the trade union for many years. She would have made a good politician. And she kept on at me to make sure that we shared the household chores. But I did them anyway. It was not a problem. Only once did each of us get really furious with the other, but that was all. She was angry and upset when I had told our youngest girl that she had an ugly mug. I'd only said it as a joke, but she was very put out and told Elvira. Although she realised that I hadn't meant it seriously, she said that girls have a tough enough time as it is. And she was right. Then Elvira infuriated me by staying away for a whole night once without any warning. She had been at a meeting which had run late and had slept on the sofa in the room behind the kitchen in the café. She had the key. And she saw my side then too, so we were never really angry. Not even when we had no money. Somehow we always got by.

"Elvira knew almost everything about flowers. When we were out walking she would know the names of all of the ones we saw. Even if we stopped outside a flower shop, she could identify them all and where they came from. But the great thing was that she was able to describe their scent as well. Then when I leaned forward to sniff, it was spot on. I think that's fantastic. To be able to describe a smell with words. But she could.

"It was pure chance that Elvira and I got to know each other. But I'm glad it happened."

◆

June 3. We spend all day on the bus driving through Germany. It's more than twenty-five degrees. Oskar sits by the window. I've never seen such big fields as here. In the evening we get to Hamburg.

June 4. Today it's even hotter. We drive around and look at various things in Hamburg before we go on. Today I sit by the window.

June 5.

June 6.

June 7. Now we're in Vienna. It's a beautiful city. It's hot and we've been out to a big palace. We walked in the park. There was also a place there with all sorts of animals.

June 8. Today it was almost too hot to go outside. But we've walked around the city looking at things. We've sent postcards home to the children.

◆

The notes that Oskar throws away.

◆

"When we were doing the housework, the vacuum cleaner would sometimes go on the blink. Then we would both take it apart and mend it. Or when we were making supper we would both be in the kitchen. And one of us did the dishes while the other cooked. It was never a problem.

"We voted the same because we thought the same. We changed party at the same time.

"We always had a good time at Christmas. The children got presents, but Elvira and I didn't give each other anything. We sang songs with the kids and danced around the Christmas tree. I expect we made a terrible racket. But we had fun. And the kids learned to be happy at home. I think that's important at a certain age. To feel welcome where you live."

The summer of 1967. The story continues. Oskar is sitting in the cabin with the summer cane lying across his blue work trousers. He has become more tired, older. When he can't solve a game of Patience, he just leaves the cards scattered on the table. Instead of getting up and going over to the work-top for the coffee pot and the spirit stove, he asks me to make the coffee. The newspapers lie unread. The smell of old age gets stronger.

◆

Few words.

Long pauses.

◆

He spends more and more time on the bench outside the house looking out over the water. Once when I come over, he is sitting there even though it is raining.

"Don't you think we should go in?"

"I seem to have got stuck here."

We go in. He is wet, but he does not put on any warm clothes.

"I never get a cold anyway. Never have. But we must have some coffee. Will you get it?"

The coffee cup between index finger and thumb. Long slurping mouthfuls. The lump of sugar on the tongue.

"I've started taking sugar in my coffee this winter. I don't know why. Doesn't make it taste any better."

More and more forgetful.

◆

Unless I've got this completely wrong.

◆

But I'm not so sure.

I don't remember anymore.

It's not important when it happened.

It doesn't matter what he was called.

◆

The eyes have dulled. Their whites have become grey. The movements are more sluggish. Head bent forward more and more.

"You really wonder what's going on. We have all these international organisations. Such as the U.N. And in spite of that we have situations like the one in Greece. Or in Spain. Or anywhere else. I read last winter that they still punish thieves by cutting off their arms and hands and feet. I look at my own stump and it's all a mystery to me. How can this be possible? Haven't we come any further than that? I remember there was someone who was executed in Sweden in about 1910. But then they put a stop to that and we thought it would be the same everywhere. It was a robber who'd killed someone. But I can't remember what he was called."

"Wasn't his name Ander?"

"What?"

"Ander?"

"Yes. Perhaps. I don't remember. Was it him?"

"Might have been."

"I see. Was he related to the balloonist?"

"That one was called Andrée."

"Right. Then there was someone by the name of Strindberg."

"He was one of them. Nils Strindberg. He was the first to die."

"How do they know?"

"That's what they think."

"I see."

"Yes."

"But I haven't lost heart. My guess is that you'll see this whole society blow apart, in one single blast. And then you can give them all my regards."

Later on, just before I go.

"I don't think I'm going to get much older than this. That's how it feels."

◆

Nowadays we usually only put out the nets one night a week. But sometimes Oskar livens up and then we are out every evening and every morning.

"One has to pull oneself together. Otherwise I fear one ends up just sitting around and moaning like the rest of them."

◆

In one single blast.

And give them my regards.

The Summer of 1968

The summer of 1968. The last one.

"How have you been this winter?"

"Not too bad. Much as ever. Been sitting in front of the T.V."

"I'm sure."

"I keep busy with this and that. But I go to bed earlier now. I get tired quickly."

"I see."

"I didn't really think I was going to come out here this year."

"Really?"

"Not that I didn't feel like it, but I do get tired. Then I decided I would come out anyway."

"It's nice to be here."

"It is. Shall we have coffee?"

"I'd love some."

"Will you make it?"

"Of course."

"You'll have to get some water first, I think"

"The bucket isn't empty yet."

"Don't bother then."

"Do you still take sugar?"

"I do. Bring us rusks while you're at it. Or there's buns if you'd like."

"A rusk will do."

"They're good. But my teeth are giving me grief."

"Are they hurting you?"

"My three teeth? Not bloody likely. But they wobble around in my mouth. I can't really bite properly."

"Have you thought about dentures?"

"No. There's no point."

"Isn't there?"

"No. I can't be bothered."

"You've bought a new pack of cards."

"The old ones were looking bloody awful. They kept sticking together. They were cheap."

"I think Öberg is now the only make."

"Really?"

"I've never seen any others."

"Is that right? It's boiling now."

"I'll turn it off."

"The radio's become a bit dodgy."

"In what way?"

"It makes a scratchy noise. The sound's so bad now I don't turn it on all that often."

"When did you come out this year?"

"About three weeks ago. It's been cold."

"Have you been in the boat at all?"

"It's leaking. I was hoping you could help me."

"Let's go out tomorrow."

"Do you think we'll get any fish?"

"I don't see why not."

"We're bound to catch something."

"Are there any people out here yet?"

"I haven't seen any. It's a while yet before the holidays. Thanks for the postcard, by the way."

"Oh, you got it."

"It was just about the only mail I got this winter. But I had a bit of difficulty reading what you wrote."

"Was it so unclear?"

"It must be my eyes."

"Have they got worse?"

"Definitely worse, I'd say. But I'm not complaining."

"The card was from London."

"Blimey."

"I spent a few weeks there."

"I see."

"It was nice."

"Good."

◆

Coffee, coffee. Long, hot gulps.

◆

"There's a lot going on."

"Yes. It's good what's happening."

"There've been demonstrations everywhere."

"I've seen them on T.V. Bloody police."

"They're rough."

"I'd have liked to have been there. They'd think twice about beating up a disabled person."

"Maybe."

"It puts me in a good mood. You'd be up for it, wouldn't you?"

"Of course."

"That's good. I've bought paint for the boat. Apparently, there's some kind of plastic in it which stops the leaking."

"Let's deal with that tomorrow."

"It'd be good if you could help me."

"Shall we put out the nets tomorrow?"

"Will the paint be dry by then?"

"I think so."

"I've been doing some mending on the nets. But they're starting to get a bit fragile."

"Let's see if I can buy some at auction this summer."

"That might be good."

"They don't usually cost all that much."

"Shall we have some more?"

"I'll pour it."

"That's enough."

"It's lovely to be out again."

"Yes. It is."

"Still a little cold though."

"Let's see how it turns out."

"Shall we take a look at the roof again this year?"

"We probably ought to. The winters can be harsh out here. And the bed is broken."

"Is it? What happened?"

"If you look underneath, you'll see that the steel springs have come unstuck in one place. Perhaps you can prop it up with a plank of some sort."

"I'll do that. Have you bought a new blanket?"

"I brought one with me from town. My boy dropped it off. They'd bought some new ones for themselves."

"Sounds good."

"I like the green."

"It's time for me to go back to my place now. But we'll see each other tomorrow."

"Let's do that. Will you take the coffee pot off the stove?"

"I'll get some water too. Is there a lot in the well?"

"There is."

"See you then."

"Yes. Bye."

"I'll bring the water right away. Where's the rope?"

"It's lying on the lid of the well."

◆

Step across the cold ground of the island. Lift the lid of the well and look down into the brown water. Lower the bucket, watch it fill up. Go back to the cabin, set the grey bucket down on the floor inside the door. Oskar is sitting on the chair with his cane across his knees. He is wearing a tattered grey sweater over his shirt.

"See you tomorrow then. Bye."

"Bye."

◆

Summer is approaching. Oskar Johansson, 1888–1969.

The Recollections

The yellow trams.
  The finger tracing a line across the wallpaper.
  The canal builder Johannes Johansson.
  Elly's white dress.
  Elvira's white dress.

◆

I played the same games as all the others.
  I've been a worker all my life.
  Everything has changed, but not for us.

◆

It's going to blow apart in one single blast.
  And give them my regards.

The Summer Cane

Oskar goes up the hill behind the house to relieve himself. He has a roll of toilet paper in his left hand. He unbuttons and lowers his trousers behind a juniper bush and squats and strains and holds himself up on his summer cane. The mosquitoes bounce off his bare skin. He looks intently at the heather and his excrement falls to the ground. He wipes himself, gets up, buttons his trousers and bends down to pick up the used paper. Then he goes back down to the house and puts the paper in the plastic bag with the rubbish.

◆

Goes in.
    Shuts the door.
    Takes a few steps.
    Props his cane up against the chair.
    Sits down on the edge of the bed.
    Straightens the sheet and the pillow
    Lies down.
    Breathes out.
    Rests.
    Looks around the room, imagines the paraffin lamp lit up
    Imagines the spirit stove burning

Imagines the static hissing from the radio.

A fishing boat passes.

The wind rises.

Distant aeroplanes.

Oskar in his cabin. Grey light.

◆

Sometimes he lies down in his grave and looks. Looks at the earth being scattered by the priest as it thuds onto his face. The wood of the coffin and the skin of his face merge. The eye becomes one with a blue surface, far away. A seagull wings its way across the blue, cutting a movement against a background of blue.

Gulls cry in the distance.

◆

Sometimes Oskar will lie there and put on a death scene. He imagines the design of the stage and gives all the directions. The tears in his eye bring a little smile to his lips as he gropes his way further and further into his dream. The index finger drums on the bed-cover. The light turns to grey.

◆

Soon the narrator will be there, but first just a few more dreams.

◆

Elvira comes in through the door.

Elvira goes out through the door.

Dreams, dreams.

Oskar's dreams.

How many were there? How many did he dream while awake? How many times did he lie down on his bed to dream, in the afternoon silence when no-one was at home?

Many.

Many.

◆

The images are clear. Clear as a flash in his eyes. Oskar is dreaming with eyes open.

◆

He is standing in the midst of the demonstrators who are marching past the leader of the revolution. He holds up a picture with one face among millions of others. He calls out.

The face trembles. The lips are drawn up towards the cheeks. Flashing teeth. A thousand faces.

Millions of white teeth.

El pueblo te defiende . . .

The people will defend you!

La revolución. A feminine noun. Woman giving birth to the future. Oskar's face among those of others.

His face among those of others. He is lying on his bed in his cabin. It is chilly. He is alone in his archipelago. He is dreaming about his revolution.

◆

The most important dream. The recurring one.

179

Then all the other ones. About Elly.

About Elvira.

About children falling over steep drops.

About work.

About the accident he never experienced but was a victim of.

About white dresses.

About fish flapping around in the bottom of a green hard-board boat.

◆

Oskar knows his dreams. He keeps them on a leash. He knows his reality. Oskar is a man who has made thousands of choices. He never got confused. He has avoided chaos. He has chosen. Whether he has made the right choices is another matter. But with his hand in Elvira's, Oskar has always made choices. Opted for, against, then for again. Chosen an allegiance, decided against it, decided in favour.

◆

The images that brush against his skin, embedded in the scent of an old man. Before the end of the road. The stump of an arm lying on his chest, rising and falling, rising and falling.

◆

He is lying in his sauna. The dreams are jostling for space. He is drawing closer.

And he asks the narrator to give his regards.

"What I liked in those days, and still do, is the way socialism battles solitude. We headed to the left and the further we went the more crowded the ranks became. That's how I met Elvira, after all. But now I look in the papers and there are whole pages full of notices in which people are falling on their knees, begging for companionship. And to think that this country has a so-called socialist government. Every one of those notices is terrible. People are so lonely. They say that their financial situation is good or bad, they identify themselves as male or female, they talk about their interests and they're on their knees pleading for companionship. Where the hell did socialism go? There was a time when we marched together. When we wanted change for the benefit of us all. It was almost like a contest without competition. Everyone wanted to give something to the person walking next to them, whom they hardly knew, but that never mattered. There was a time when we were happy to see someone new join the march, someone we hadn't seen before. But nowadays people tend to get annoyed if someone new turns up. What the hell is he doing here? Is he a threat to my position?

"It's bad.

"What do I care if they have long hair? All that matters is that they're out there, marching and creating a racket. They're more than welcome to smell like shit as far as I'm concerned, just so long as they're there.

"And if they were to throw stones through the windows of my boy's laundry business, then that's probably just as it should be. And you can quote me on that.

"I've heard people say that they've seen enough workers to stop them believing in the revolution. To which I say, or used to say: I'm amazed at how many mirrors you have hanging on the wall at home.

"I don't know if they understood what I meant. I hope they did, because they were just talking crap."

◆

What happened to it? Oskar ducks the answer. He knows, he knows perfectly well. But he feels guilty and then the extent of his own involvement becomes unclear and uncertain. Time and again he blurts out: one single blast. And give my regards.

◆

My name is Oskar.

Johansson, former rock blaster.

"I don't have much in the way of hands, but I can still pitch in. And I know I look bloody awful with just one eye, but at least I can see."

My name is Oskar.

I'm not afraid of you.

I'll tell you what I think of you.

You can call me whatever you like.

One day you'll see.

The summer cane bangs hard against the table leg. He drops it and I bend down and hand it to him.

"One does get angry. That must be the last thing that goes."

♦

Oskar. The unremarkable. Johansson in the trade union register. Johansson to the bosses. Johansson on his pension slip. Johansson to the election campaign organisers. Johansson to everybody.

"I do have a king's name but you must admit that it also sounds like thunder."

"Johansson is a good name. People understand it over the telephone without my having to spell it. And nobody gets it wrong."

♦

One "s" or two?

Does it matter?

♦

"I'm sure I still have our passport from the coach trip somewhere. It was a joint one for Elvira and me. The photographs were hilarious. Elvira looked as if she had a whole egg in her mouth. She wanted the pictures to be taken again, but I told her we shouldn't be vain. Or should I put some lipstick on my left eye?"

♦

The dreams are red.

The cane bangs against the table leg.

Oskar is more than seventy years old.

♦

"El *pueblo te defiende*. I don't know what it means, but when you see the photographs you get the message."

"If you look, you'll see."

"Can you see the power of it?"

"They have demands."

◆

"Did you see?"

"Did you see?"

"What they want is a better life."

"You can take the paper with you if you want to read it. I know what it says."

"Half past four tomorrow, then."

"Bring some sugar if you have any."

◆

"There are lots of flies."

"Half past four tomorrow, then. I'll have coffee for you."

Oskar Johansson 1888–1969

Autumn, winter, spring. 1968–9.

◆

Oskar leaves the island at the end of October. The oak trees are bare and there is snow in the air. The boat comes to pick him up at ten o'clock. The engine thuds and the man helps Oskar with his suitcase. Oskar closes the door, locks it and puts the key into his pocket. He is wearing a grey overcoat and a hat. The fisherman helps him into the boat. Oskar sits on a bench down in the cargo hold. All you can see sticking out is his hat and part of his forehead.

The boat backs out, turns and disappears around the headland.

It is a Sunday. His son is there to meet him at the harbour on the mainland. Oskar settles into the back seat of the large American car. It vanishes up the hill. The gravel is hard and cold under the wheels.

◆

He sits at the kitchen table in his apartment on the ground floor. It is quiet. Distant sounds from the street barely touch him. The kitchen clock ticks. It is a quarter past seven. He has his coffee cup in front of him. A plate with rusks. A packet of milk. The wax tablecloth is beige. The winter cane, the black one, is lying on the table.

He turns his head and looks straight at us. There is a scraping from the letter box and a thud against the hall mat. He gets up, takes his cane and starts to walk out of the kitchen. He keeps close to the wall. He brushes past the sink, the cleaning cupboard, the doorpost, and he bends down to pick up a whole lot of papers of different colours scattered all over the floor by the front door. Then he hobbles back to the kitchen. When he bends down, he squeezes the cane into his right armpit and presses it firmly against his body. Then he swaps over, puts the pieces of paper under his armpit and holds the cane with his finger and thumb.

◆

He is sitting by the kitchen table and looking through the day's post. All advertising leaflets. He looks at them, one by one.

◆

Some of them.

◆

Algots' autumn range. Young people in stiff poses, prancing about in variously coloured empty rooms. Cold, forbidding tones. The pictures show them jumping around in grotesque capers and challenging Oskar with looks that say:

♦

Buy me.

Be warm and safe this autumn.

Buy me.

Buy me.

♦

This week's special at Domus. Delicious broilers, rock-bottom prices.

♦

The stencil is messy and blurred.

And don't miss the chance to visit our sports department. Our winter range offers many exciting novelties.

Oskar on skis.

Oskar on skates.

Oskar on a winter walk.

♦

A.B.F.'s adult education programme.

Our mission statement is . . .

Needlework or English.

Creative Drama or university-level Spanish.

♦

With the course booklet in hand, Oskar looks out of the window. The dustbin lorry thunders past.

♦

I buy my own food.

I do my own laundry. There isn't that much of it.

I do my own cleaning.

◆

Then he sits in front of the television and looks at a school programme. High school physics. He watches intently. He nods when he has understood. He does not think that all is long over and done with. He is still very much a part of it, Oskar Johansson, even though he is now nearly eighty.

◆

His birthday. The newspaper says he is turning eighty. But there is no picture.

They sit around the table in the living room. Two large cakes have been cut. Steam rises from coffee cups. Oskar is wearing a white shirt and a tie and a black jacket. The children are sitting there, all three of them, the daughters with their husbands and the son with his wife. They chat among themselves while Oskar sits and listens. The presents are on the table.

A grey pullover. A pair of slippers. Sunglasses, polarised ones.

◆

Or. Oskar sits alone at the kitchen table, wearing his blue work trousers. The coffee cup, the rusks and the glass of milk. He is turning eighty.

◆

Or back to the previous scene.

"Would you like more coffee, Pappa?"

"I've had enough thanks."

"Go on, have some more. It's your birthday after all."

"A little more then."

"You're looking so well. Have you had a good summer?"

"Yes."

"Have you heard that I'm going to open a branch in the town where she lives?" The son points at one of his sisters.

"Blimey."

"That would make it my third one."

"And is business good?"

"It is. So far, at any rate."

The camera's flash cuts through the room. The son is taking pictures. The daughters sit on either side of Oskar. Then it is time for them to leave. They get up, smooth down their dresses, straighten their hair with the palms of their hands. Smile and laugh. Bend down for a quick hug. Straighten their hair again.

"Thanks, Pappa. You take care now."

"Thanks to you too."

"We'll write soon."

"Drive carefully."

The door closes. It's quiet. The clock ticks. Oskar goes and lies down on the bed. He is tired. He looks straight up at the ceiling.

◆

The days.

◆

The coffee pot. The rusks. The morning newspaper.

The advertising leaflets. The occasional letter or postcard.

Do some housework, stay clean. Sit in front of the television.

Lunch. Coffee again.

Shop if necessary. Rummage around in drawers. Straighten a mat.

Sit by the window.

Television. Coffee again.

Undress. Lie and look at the ceiling. Sleep, sleep.

◆

"Of course I suffered and felt stupid and lonely because of my injuries. If I hadn't met Elvira, I don't know what I would have done. I couldn't bear to see myself in a mirror and I was revolted by the sight of my mutilated arm. Then I also got that weird sensation. That I sort of felt my right hand even though it wasn't there. It was dreadful. Some nights I would dream that everything was as it should be and then I'd wake up in the morning and begin to scream and go all funny. If I hadn't had Elvira, I don't know how things would have turned out. I kept myself to myself and in some way felt embarrassed. But I didn't give up. I learned quite quickly to get by with my finger and thumb. It's not as hard as people think. It seems difficult when you're imagining it, but when you actually have to do it, it works itself out. It must be worse to be blind or deaf.

"But I don't know how I would have managed without Elvira. She gave me self-confidence, which is what I needed. Not pity, but kicks up the backside. In any case you get used to it. After four or five years I never again felt awkward because of my handicap. You see, there was just so much else that was important at the time, as I've told you. It was not until I got old and Elvira passed away that I started getting irritable again. But I suppose that was because my body was beginning to give out in other ways too. I don't feel that I've been handicapped, though. That's not how it seemed to me. Ever. And I was just as ugly before it happened. Although of course I'd never wish all this on anyone else. When I read about accidents where people have been maimed in different ways, or when I see what the bombs can do, I know what it's like for the victims. And not everybody is lucky enough to meet an Elvira straight afterwards. But there was always something else which was more important. And there still is, I suppose, but gradually I'm beginning to be out of it. Old age isn't much fun. You become a different sort of underdog. There's so much one has to put up with. But one always manages.

"Much is to Elvira's credit. But my character and my convictions were also important. I still hold those beliefs, but there's a limit to what one can do.

"At least I don't talk aloud to myself. Many lonely people do. I wonder what they have to say to themselves. I hope it's something fun.

"If I was young, I'm sure I'd do it all again. I would certainly have believed in the same cause. There's nothing extraordinary about socialism, let's face it. Once you've worked out how everything hangs together, it's actually obvious. Then everything else is wrong and strange. Is there anything more crazily illogical and unreasonable than capitalism? I don't think so.

"Socialism is nothing special. And neither am I. So we probably go well together. Elvira sometimes said that she thought we did. And then she laughed, of course. As always.

"I wouldn't want to have been born as anything else. That's not what matters, after all.

"Whether you like it or not, you're a part of it. Just spit into the ocean once. And then you have all the eternity you need."

◆

Oskar.

A strange old boy who lives in an old army sauna.

He usually waves when you go by. He's only got one hand and one eye.

You should see his index finger. It's this thick.

He probably sits out there, drinking akvavit. It must be an awful mess. Who tidies up after him? And I suspect he never washes.

I wonder who owns the land he's living on.

He's a great old man. He used to be a rock blaster and had a terrible accident. But he's a cheerful soul anyhow. He's a nice old boy. And he looks after himself. He's happy in his sauna, they say.

◆

Oskar on the ground floor.

Oskar's son owns that big laundry business, you know the one?

He has two girls, too.

His wife is dead.

He turned eighty just recently.

He does his own shopping.

◆

"He walks with a cane."

◆

"But he's so handicapped."

◆

"He always says hello."

◆

"I hear him when he takes out the rubbish."

◆

In the middle of November, he is admitted to hospital and his right leg is amputated. It is the only way they can stop the gangrene. He lies in his white bed and a few days before Christmas he suffers his first stroke. It paralyses him and he cannot talk. In the afternoon on Christmas Eve his children come to visit him. They stand around the bed. Oskar looks at them. His mouth has become locked in a stiff smile. They pat his cheek, stroke his hair, touch his two fingers. Then they leave the ward.

♦

Poor Pappa.

"Let's hope he won't have to lie there too long."

"It would be best if he could die."

"Some go on like that for ten years. He has a strong heart, after all."

"There's hardly anything left of him."

"It's terrible to see."

"We must be prepared for him to die at any moment."

"We must call each other."

"I'll come back here as soon as I can."

Out through the hospital entrance. Bare ground, Christmas Eve. Darkness falls.

"Happy Christmas, then. Love to everyone."

"You too."

"And we'll call."

"Yes. Where do you need to go? I can give you a lift."

"You don't have to."

"My car is right over here."

♦

The assistant nurse is sitting by the bed, feeding him. It is Christmas Eve.

♦

The second stroke comes one day in April. The bowl of porridge tips over onto his chest and Oskar is dead.

Afterwards

The spring of 1971.

I have an errand in town. I arrive in the morning and am only staying for a few hours.

Before I catch my train back, I have time to go into a pub by the station and drink a beer.

The place is packed. Smoky and the sour smell of beer.

The darts whirl through the smoke and hit the board. Clattering, glasses, jostling.

◆

Oskar is dead.

And now for the future.

◆

Exactly as he said.

Afterword

It is 1972, and Henning Mankell learns that his novel *Bergsprängaren* has been accepted for publication. His first book. Writing about the international political situation at the time, he explains that "I remember what I was thinking. It was a time of great joy, of great energy. Everything was still possible. Nothing was either lost or settled. Except that the Vietnamese were certain to win. Imperialism was beginning to show signs of strain."

The book is a modern "Everyman", the story of an ordinary life filled with the usual triumphs and tragedies, great and small, set against the major Swedish and international political developments of the twentieth century. Oskar Johansson experiences some directly, others at a distance, but he does not believe that he has had anything to do with the changes that have taken place in Sweden during his lifetime. They have happened, and they have had an effect, but he feels he has played no role in their coming about.

In 1997, twenty-five years later, *Bergsprängaren* is republished, and Mankell adds a preface: "Certainly, much has happened in those twenty-five years. Some walls have come down, others have gone up. One empire has fallen, the other is being been weakened from within, new centres of power are taking shape. But the poor and exploited have become even poorer during these years. And Sweden has gone from making an honest attempt at building a decent society to social depredation. An ever-clearer division between those who are needed and those who are expendable. Today there are ghettos outside Swedish cities. Twenty-five years ago they did not exist.

"As I read through this book again after all these years, I realise that this quarter century has been but a short time in history. What I wrote here is still highly relevant.

"I have made a number of small changes to the wording for this edition. But the story is the same. I have not touched it. It was not necessary to do so."

And now, in 2020, almost another "short time in history" after Mankell wrote his preface, *Bergsprängaren* is finally published in English as *The Rock Blaster*. What would Mankell say about it today?

Of course, the global political landscape has hardly improved. Migration, a significant issue ever since the end of the Second World War, has been brought into sharp focus as immigration, and the Swedish ghettos of which he wrote in 1997 have seen frequent unrest. Populism, misinformation and the weakening of liberal democratic values, which loom ever larger in our lives, would attract his strong criticism. His socialist heart would be no less saddened by the current state of social democracy in Sweden. What he wrote concerning the rise and fall of empires has been borne out, and the disparity between wealth and poverty has continued to grow, exacerbated by the dominance of corporate giants. And what would he make of climate change and the threat to our physical environment?

Oskar's reality, according to Mankell, is a matter of the struggle between capitalism and socialism, between revolution and reformism. We know on whose side both he and Oskar stand in the first. But that battle is no longer the main one that divides our world – the primary focus now is not on left versus right, but on the growing authoritarianism in many societies; and nobody speaks of "imperialism", in the sense that Mankell meant it, any more.

As for the second struggle, however intense both Oskar and Mankell's longing for revolution – a longing fuelled by their disappointment in what Oskar calls social democracy's "greatest outrage", the fact that it "turned socialism into some sort of organisation for unnecessary civil servants to line their pockets at the expense of the workers" – in practice they are both reformers. Yes, Oskar is happy every time there is a revolution somewhere on the globe. And yes, he expects, and wants, "this whole society" to be blown apart (appropriately enough). But his contribution will merely be to "give them all my regards". Confronted by Sergeant Lindholm at the Nazi rally in Humlegården, he does not take action, he can only "imagine himself charging in and jabbing his finger and thumb into the Sergeant's face".

Yet one hopes that Mankell would still consider what he wrote in The Rock Blaster "highly relevant". Because Oskar is Everyman, whether he or the narrator (Is it Mankell? I think not) are right about whether he played a role in bringing about the social changes of the twentieth century. As most of us are. Ordinary people standing in the storm. And that is what makes *The Rock Blaster* such an engaging book, especially in a world as challenging and bewildering as ours today.

G.G., JANUARY 2020

Glossary of Swedish Terms, People, Places and Organisations

"20 Frågor", long-running radio programme based on the game "Twenty Questions". Panellists have included the author Astrid Lindgren.

A.B.F., Arbetarnas bildningsförbund ("Workers' Educational Association"), which offers its members a wide range of courses, study groups and seminars.

Algots, Swedish manufacturer of ready-to-wear clothes, which it sold chiefly through the Co-operative Federation. Founded in 1907 by Algot Johansson, it went bankrupt in 1977.

Andrée, Solomon August (1954–97), attempted to reach the North Pole in a balloon in 1897, together with Knut Frænkel and Nils Strindberg. The expedition failed and, after a number of weeks travelling across the ice, all members of the expedition died.

Axbom, Sven (1926–2006), Swedish footballer born near Norrköping (the city of Oskar's birth) who played in every Swedish match in the 1958 World Cup.

Danielsson, Axel (1863–99), Swedish left-wing journalist and activist who, together with Hjalmar Branting (q.v.), was convicted of blasphemy for one of his articles.

Bergegren, Hinke (1861–1936), Swedish politician who was an early member of the Social Democratic Party but whose particular views (anarcho-syndicalist, pro-birth control) led to his expulsion from the party and a short prison sentence. He subsequently joined the Communist Party.

Branting, Hjalmar (1860–1925), Swedish politician. He was a long-serving chairman of the Social Democratic Party, and became prime minister three times (notably the first from that party). Joint winner of the Nobel Peace Prize in 1921.

"Bombing raids" – given the date (1968), this is likely to be a reference to the U.S.'s aerial bombardment campaign in Vietnam nicknamed "Operation Rolling Thunder", which began in March 1965 and ended on 2 November 1968.

Boren, lake in central southern Sweden which forms a part of the Göta Canal (q.v.).

"Cocktail", Swedish soft-porn magazine published from the 1940s until the 1970s.

"Dagens Eko" (often referred to by its abbreviated name "Ekot"), the main news programme broadcast by Swedish Radio.

Dahl, Richard (1933–2007), Swedish athlete whose career highlight was his unexpected victory in the high jump at the European Athletics Championships in Stockholm in 1958.

Domö, Fritiof (1889–1961), Swedish conservative politician, government minister and leader of the Moderate Party.

Domus, brand name of the department stores operated by the Swedish Cooperative Union between 1956 and 2012.

"El pueblo te defiende" – "The people will defend you"; supporters of Salvador Allende, president of Chile 1970–3, are said to have chanted this as they marched past the presidential palace in Santiago in a demonstration some days before the coup which toppled him and led to his death.

Elfsborg Fortress, also known as **Älvsborg** Fortress, originally lay on the Swedish mainland near Göteborg. In the seventeenth century, a new fortress was built on a small island off the Göteborg coast. The eponymous chapbook song that Oskar sings was written by August Wilhelm Thorsson in the 1880s. It is suitably melodramatic and concerns a lonely prisoner in Älvsborg, and the death of his lover in a rowing boat in the mouth of the Göta River during a night-time storm, right by the fortress.

Engberg, Arthur (1888–1944), Swedish social democratic politician and government minister.

Erlander, Tage (1901–85), Swedish politician, chairman of the Social Democratic Party and prime minister following the death of Per Albin Hansson (q.v.).

Far – Swedish for "father".

Farfar – Swedish for a paternal grandfather, literally "father's father".

Farsan – informal and affectionate Swedish word for one's father, equivalent to "Dad" or (when talking to others) "my/the old man".

"Forum", current affairs programme launched on Swedish radio in 1969 and later transferred to Swedish television.

Göta Canal, a 190-km long waterway consisting of canal sections, lakes and rivers, which was constructed 1810–32 to link Göteborg and the Baltic Sea.

Hagberg, Hilding (1899–1993), Swedish communist politician and leader of the Communist Party.

Hansson, Per Albin (1885–1946), Swedish politician, chairman of the Social Democratic Party. In 1932, he became the first of the party's prime ministers during its forty-four-year period in government. He was one of the major influences in the building of a socialist Sweden after the Second World War.

Harstena, island in the middle of the Baltic Sea, used as one of the reference locations for the shipping forecasts broadcast by Swedish Radio.

Hermansson, Carl-Henrik "C.-H." (1917–2016), Swedish communist and politician. He was chairman of the Swedish Communist Party (1964–75) and among those responsible for turning it away from Stalinism.

Humlegården, a park and garden in the centre of Stockholm which houses the Royal Library and a monument to the botanist and zoologist Carl von Linné (Linnaeus).

Hyland, Lennart (1919–1993), Swedish television host and personality best known for the talk show "Hylands hörna" ("Hyland's corner"), which ran from 1962 to 1983.

Katarina Bangata, street in the Södermalm district of Stockholm, originally intended as a stretch of railway line.

Kilbom, Karl (1885–1961), Swedish socialist politician. He was a member of the Communist Party until he was expelled, after which he became an active member of the Social Democratic Party.

"King Oskar", King Oscar II of Sweden and Norway (1829–1907, reigned 1872–1907). The king himself always spelled his name with a "c", but practice varies. On page [185], Oskar says this: "I do have a king's name but you must admit that it also sounds like thunder" – *åska* (the Swedish word for thunder) is pronounced almost the same as "Oskar".

Kreuger, Ivar (1880–1932), Swedish entrepreneur and creator of the business that eventually became Swedish Match, which sells tobacco, cigars, matches and more. His empire collapsed at the beginning of the 1930s, during the depression; his death was declared a suicide, but his family and others have maintained that he was murdered.

"Kriminaljournalen", a now defunct men's magazine containing sensationalised stories and some soft-porn images.

"Lansen", the Saab 32 Lansen, a Swedish military jet aircraft produced during the late 1950s.

Lidköping, small town in south-west Sweden.

Moberg, Vilhelm (1898-1973), Swedish journalist and author whose best-known books are the four-part "Emigrants" series written in the 1950s, which deals with a southern Swedish family forced by economic circumstance to emigrate to the U.S. in the mid-nineteenth century. The story inspired a 1971 film starring Max von Sydow and Liv Ullmann.

Mor – an informal and affectionate Swedish word for one's mother, equivalent to "Mum".

Norrköping, in eastern central Sweden, is the closest city to Oskar's birthplace, about 160 km from Stockholm and with easy access to the Baltic Sea via the Bråviken Bay.

Öberg, full name A.B. J.O. Öberg & Son, a business conglomerate established in 1845. Its businesses produced playing cards and printed office products; after a number of acquisitions, it became part of the Esselte Group in 1985.

Ögonblick – Swedish for "a moment".

Palm, August (1849–1922), by trade a tailor, was a social democratic activist and agitator.

Palme, Olof (1927–86), Swedish politician, leader of the Social Democratic Party and twice prime minister (1969–76 and

1982–86). He was assassinated in Stockholm in 1986. His murder has never been solved, despite extensive investigations.

Pappa – Swedish for "father", also a form of address equivalent to "Father" or "Daddy".

Pehrsson-Bramstorp, Axel (1883–1954), Swedish politician and briefly prime minister (from June to September 1936). Born Axel Pehrsson, he came from a well-to-do farming family, and was associated with – and later adopted the name of – the Bramstorp family, whose farm in southern Sweden he acquired.

"Outer archipelago" – Oskar's island seems to have been a part of the Östergötland archipelago, which lies in the Baltic Sea approximately 60 km south of the Bråviken Bay near Norrköping. The archipelago is about 5 km offshore at its furthest point.

Radio Nord, a Swedish commercial radio station which broadcast from international waters in the Baltic Sea off Stockholm during the early 1960s.

Sköld, Per Edvin (1891–1972), Swedish social democratic politician and government minister.

"Snurran", family-oriented radio programme which broadcast 1953–58 (and briefly in 1962), after which it transferred to Swedish Television.

Social Democratic Party, founded in 1889. It is the oldest and largest political party in Sweden, and was in power for extensive periods of time during the twentieth century.

Söderköping, a small town about 15 km south-east of Norrköping. Its historical significance is greater than its current standing – it was the site of two royal coronations.

Söderman, August (1832–76), Swedish composer of the Romantic period.

"Sons of Labour" (Swedish: "Arbetets söner") was a popular song in the labour movement in Sweden, first sung in the mid-1880s.

Strindberg, Nils (1872–97), one of three balloonists who died in 1897 while trying to reach the North Pole; see also "Andrée, Solomon August".

Svensson, Kalle (1925–2000), nicknamed Rio-Kalle. Swedish goalkeeper who played in seventy-three matches for the Swedish national team. His last international match was the 1958 World Cup final against Brazil, which Sweden lost 5–2.

Syndicalism, a radical and significant early twentieth-century European socialist movement, which focused on the local organisation of workers and on strike action.

Tingsten, Herbert (1896–1973), Swedish political scientist and journalist. He was, among other things, the editor of "Dagens Nyheter", one of Sweden's two main national daily newspapers, from 1946 to 1959.

Undén, Östen (1886–1974), Swedish professor of civil law, and social democratic politician and government minister.

von Sydow, Oscar Fredrik (1973–1936), Swedish independent politician, government minister and, for a brief period in 1921, prime minister.

Wigforss, Ernst (1881–1977), Swedish social democratic politician and government minister.

HENNING MANKELL (1948–2015) became a international phenomenon with his crime writing, gripping thrillers and atmospheric novels set in Africa. His prizewinning and critically acclaimed Inspector Wallander mysteries dominated bestseller lists all over the world. His books have been translated into forty-five languages and adapted numerous times for film and television.

GEORGE GOULDING's translations from the Swedish include *The Girl in the Spider's Web*, *The Girl Who Takes an Eye for an Eye*, *The Girl Who Lived Twice* and *Fall of Man in Wilmslow*, all by David Lagercrantz, and *The Carrier* by Mattias Berg.